Jessica's Secret Journal

By

Meo Rose

This book is a work of fiction. Places, events, and situations in this story are purely fictional. Any resemblance to actual persons, living or dead, is coincidental.

© 2004 by Meo Rose. All rights reserved.

No part of this book may be reproduced, stored in a retrieval system, or transmitted by any means, electronic, mechanical, photocopying, recording, or otherwise, without written permission from the author.

ISBN: 1-4140-0106-1 (e-book)
ISBN: 1-4140-0104-5 (Paperback)
ISBN: 1-4140-0105-3 (Dust Jacket)

Library of Congress Control Number: 2003096919

This book is printed on acid free paper.

Printed in the United States of America
Bloomington, IN

1stBooks – rev. 01/16/04

Dedicated to my mother Sylvia Rose, who is now deceased. Your voice still rings in my ears. The word CAN'T was not allowed in our family. "CAN'T never did nothing. Get busy and try." That wise advice has served me well over the years.

Acknowledgements:

Thank you to my husband Don who has been my main source of encouragement. "It's better than many I've read, and I've read a good many," were his words. I could never have done it without you.

Also:

Danese, my eldest daughter, who is bravely facing her own trauma at this time.

Ruthanne, who encouraged me to get out and fly the American skies.

Rhonda who's devotion and sacrifice for her family gives us something to work toward.

Sheri, my youngest, who should have been named Joy, because that is what she has been.

To Casey, my computer buddy, and all of my grandchildren. Love Grandmother.

Special thanks to my sister-in-law the first MEO.

I cannot leave out my friends Ollie, Linda, Avelina and others, who read my manuscript and made suggestions, I say thank-you.

Meo Rose

Chapter One

May 30, 2001

Thirty three year old Lawrence Bovier hadn't lost his temper for some time. The medication he was on was helping him. If only he hadn't lost it the last time, his mother might still be alive. She was to blame he reasoned. She had often provoked him, even when he had warned her not to. The last time he hurt her they had put him in the mental institution here in New York. He didn't mean to hurt her. They had taken him to her funeral when she died. Larry as they called him, had cried and was despondent for weeks.

Why hadn't she listened to him, he wondered? "Why didn't she just do what I asked her to do?" he said to his image in the mirror, as he combed his brown hair, and shaved the stubble on his chin. He hated his stooped shoulders, it reminded him of his grandfather Smith. Both of his grandparents were dead, and he was all alone now except for Adam Bovier, his real dad. As long as he had his medication, every one seemed to like him. He had made friends here in New York, but he always longed for more.

"Hi, Donna, ready to eat," he said to his friend, as she entered the dining room. The woman was tall and rather lanky, with brown hair falling down her back.

"Sure," the woman said. Donna needed a friend, though Larry wasn't her choice. He was insidious, she thought, and very capable of maneuvering her. She didn't want to make problems for herself because she would be leaving soon. "I'm getting out of here the first day of June," she told Larry.

"Where will you go?" Larry wanted to know.

"Oh, I don't know." Donna still had nightmares of the accident she and her husband were in over two years before. Marissa, her two year old daughter was killed at the sight, and Donna's husband, Troy lived just four days, and then died in the hospital. The guilt was overwhelming, since Donna had been driving the car. Later, she had tried to commit suicide. That's why she had been sent here. Now she was being released. The Doctor said if she would stay on her medicine, there was no reason for her to stay here. Although she felt like she wasn't ready to face the world alone. "I have no one to go home to, so I'll have to start over." she told Larry.

Donna thought about what the doctor had said. 'You can re-marry, Donna, your only thirty five, and still very pleasing to look at.' She wanted to believe him.

"Me get married?" She laughed. Troy, her husband had always called her, his little doe. That made her smile. She still missed his gentleness. The hurt was still there whenever she saw a small child. Especially a two year old girl with big blue eyes, that resembled her little Marissa.

He hadn't said she was beautiful, she knew she wasn't. She looked into her mirror. Her dark brown hair was pulled back into a bun at the base of her neck. Light brown eyes looked back at her. She had a soft look. Lipstick was something new for her. One of the other patients gave her a tube of lipstick as a farewell gift. Donna pulled out a suitcase and put the few things she had inside, and then went down for her last meal here at the New York Mental Facility.

Larry was waiting for her and handed her a tray of food. They sat at a corner table away from the others. "I'm going to help you, Donna, I have a plan," he said. Larry didn't want to lose his friend. "Will you marry me?" he asked her.

"You would marry me? What would we live on?" she asked.

"My father is rich, he'll give us money," he told her. "If he doesn't I'll find another way. I'll need your help." he said, as he planned his escape.

Donna was afraid to say no. Later that day, on June first, Donna said goodbye to her friends and was released from the State of New York Mental Facility. She took a taxi to a car rental, and rented a car and then went back for Larry. She pulled up in front of the side door. He was standing hidden by a brick pillar. He checked around and then he slipped into the seat beside her and she drove away.

"This feels naughty," she said, as she followed Larry's directions.

"We have a commission," he bellowed out a sardonic laugh.

They had drove about half and hour, when Larry motioned her over to a gas station. "We'll get gas and some food to take with us, so we can keep driving."

Donna got out and went to the restroom. A man stopped her to ask if her for directions. She couldn't help him, so she went in, and when she came out she saw him again.

"Have a good trip," she said and walked back to the car.

Larry got behind the wheel and pulled the car to the curb. He reached over and slapped Donna on her face. "Don't you talk to strangers, they could be looking for us. Don't you understand? I will never go back without you," he yelled at her.

Donna slumped in her seat and tears rolled down her cheeks.

"Now look what you made me do." Larry reached over and wiped the tears with his hand. "Let's eat, okay," he handed her a bag full of food.

Larry pointed at the sign. Boston it read. "That's us," he said and then he turned on the radio, and crooned to Donna until she fell asleep. He found them a cheap motel when they got to Boston. They called the Hatley House the next morning. Larry told Donna what to say.

"Hello," Jo Anna Bovier answered the phone.

"Hello," Donna said. "This is Donna Mavis. We are looking for work, even temporary work. My husband and I work as a team," she lied. "We wondered if you had any such work available?"

Jo Anna had called the, Temporaries earlier. James and Mary were planning a vacation. She assumed this call was from the work agency. "Yes, I did call. Please come on over tomorrow, the Morgans will show you around and get you settled in before they leave on vacation. They have a trip scheduled for the fourteenth of June. Is that going to be convenient?"

"Yes madam," Donna looked at Larry for approval.

"Good, I will tell the Morgans you will be here for training tomorrow." Jo Anna was glad to have that settled.

The next morning, they went to eat and then Larry stopped at a specialty shop. When he walked back to the car Donna laughed. He had disguised himself with dark glasses, a mustache, and a beret. She would not have recognized him if it would not have been for his slumped back. They returned the rent car, and took a taxi to the Hatley House.

"You look so funny Larry." Donna told him.

"You will call me Larry Mavis while we are here." He was taking no chances on being recognized until he was ready.

James was waiting and opened the gate for them. He showed them around the garages, and then he took them through the back door. An extra room was next to the kitchen. He showed them in and got them settled.

"I like the big black man, James," Larry told Donna when they were alone. "He took me to meet Mr. Joe Santana, and showed me his shed where he works on his plants. I saw Mr. Santana take a book from Jo Anna Bovier and carry it to the shed. I watched him lock it into a big chest, and hang the key on it's door."

"Why would you be interested in the book?" she asked Larry.

"It looked like a family album to me. I want to see for myself, the rest of this family. Can you even imagine living in this mansion?" Larry asked her.

"We are living here now." Donna joked. "She couldn't keep up with his deviousness."

"This is going to be mine someday," he smiled as he told her.

Donna was scared when he talked that way. "How will you get it?"

"I'll just take it. It should be mine anyway." Larry snapped at her. He had an envelope in his hand. It was an envelope with Jessica Moore's address written on it.

Donna had seen it in the kitchen. "What is that?" she asked him.

He glared at her. "My gold mine," he said, pushing it into her face.

"Cut it out," she told him.

Larry grabbed her arm and twisted it behind her back. "Listen here, don't you ever-ever make me hit you lady, cause I will," he snapped at her and pushed her onto the bed. Donna started to cry. Larry grabbed her shoulders and shook her. "You shut up," he said, "or I'll shut you up. Do you understand?" he said as he pushed her face into the pillow.

Donna was thankful when someone came in the back door. It was James, she could tell by his voice. Larry let her up, and then he went into the kitchen.

She heard Larry's voice. "Sure I'll walk with you."

James and Larry walked through the gardens, and when they approached the cottage, James excused himself and went to see Joe. Larry slipped into the shed and put the key on the chest door into his pocket. Before he came out he put a wedge under the side window, and then he sat down on the porch swing and waited for James.

"Well I had better lock up," Joe said as he pulled the shed door shut and turned the key.

That evening Larry waited in his room. When everything was quiet he called James on the intercom. When James answered he said. "James, this is Larry. We have an emergency in California, that we need to handle, it's a family thing. We need to fly out tomorrow. I've made a reservation for ten a.m. Could you drive us to the airport?"

"When can you be back?" James asked.

"We'll be back on the thirteenth. You can still leave on the fourteenth."

"Sounds good. Sure see you in the morning then," James went back to bed.

In the night Donna heard Larry open the door and walk outside. She fell asleep and didn't hear him when he returned. When they boarded the aircraft, the next morning, Larry wanted to sit alone. It wasn't a full flight so the attendant accommodated him. Donna could see his head two seats in front of her.

She watched as he shuffled through the scrape-book. After while he must have found what he was looking for. He left to go to the front, and Donna got up and checked on what he was reading. He had left it open on Chapter Nine.

'Lawrence Bovier' was the title. "So, he is in the book," she spoke quietly to herself. She hoped he liked what he read, or she knew she would suffer.

Donna watched with her partially closed eyes, faking sleep. Larry finally returned and asked for a bourbon and sat down to read.

This was the family he didn't know, Larry thought. 'Adam Bovier and Dorothy Smith gave birth to a son. Adam was just eighteen and Dorothy was a pretty sixteen year old. Dorothy got pregnant, and at the insistence of her parents, she and Adam got married. Rather than risk a scandal, Adam's parents agreed. From that time on Lawrence was used as a pawn. The Smiths financially bled the Boviers.

When Lawrence was five years old, Adam got a divorce. As a result Dorothy walked away with a substantial amount of money, and a son whom she spoiled in every way possible. The Smiths moved to France and Adam lost tract of his son.

When Adam turned twenty three he met Jo Anna Hatley. He fell in love and married her. Three years later they had a baby girl, just eight years after Lawrence was born.

Years passed without any news of Lawrence or his mother. Until Mr. Ash, Adam's lawyer, received a letter from Lawrence's mother Dorothy. He called Adam and told him he had heard from Dorothy. Lawrence had grown into a disturbed child and was in The State of New York Mental Institute. His grandparents had died two years before and Dorothy was ill and desolate. Dorothy had called to pled with Adam to help. "After all," she had said, "he had gotten her pregnant."

Adam had continued to send money until she died. Adam was still paying for his son's stay at the Mental Institution. He had tried to visit his son. Unfortunately, his son had been taught to hate him from infancy. He was told by the officials at the

Institute, not to visit Lawrence. After each visit, they said he became so violent, he would have to be put in restraints. As a result Adam hadn't seen his son in five years.
End of Chapter.

When Larry and Donna left the aircraft, at LAX airport, they rented a car and headed toward Long Beach. Larry found a motel near the Navar Building. "I want to keep my eye out for my half sister, Jessica Moore," he told Donna.

Chapter Two

It was a dreary day in Long Beach. But Jessica sensed more than just gloominess. "What is happening to me?" Jessica sat at her desk. She couldn't move. She was speechless. If she could talk, she wondered to whom could she talk? She had always felt safe here. For the last five years she had considered the "Long Beach Chronical" her haven. Jessica reached for the telephone book and turned to the Physician section. Her eye caught the Phyciatrist listings. Her finger followed the names-b-c-d-e—h. There it was. Dr. Malcolm Hampton. Everyone had left the office for the day except Randal Scott. She could hear him talking on the phone in his office across the hall. Jessica picked up the phone and dialed the number. She listened to it ring, as she tapped her pen nervously on the desk and took a deep breath.

"Hello, Dr. Hampton's office, may I help you?" A woman answered.

"Yes, yes I guess so," Jessica stuttered. "When can I get an appointment to see Dr. Hampton?" She heard someone leafing through a book.

"We do have a cancellation tomorrow at three o'clock p.m. What did you say your name was?" the girl asked.

"Jessica Moore, thank-you, and I'll be there at three o'clock p.m. sharp," she said, and hung up the phone.

Jessica walked to the window and parted the blinds with her finger just enough to view the wet streets below. From the tenth floor of the twenty two floors of the Namar Towers, Jessica watched as the rain spilled downward from the eves and into the gutters by the curbs below. The gray fog that hung heavy over the city added to the ominous feelings that had enveloped her today. Her breath clouded the pane of glass. She rubbed it off with the palm of her hand, and then she looked down at the dark lines that the cars made in the wet cement. She could see a small lake in the distance. On a clear day it would be filled with sail boats. Today, the water seemed black with deep currents stirring beneath, and slapping at the shoreline.

Jessica thought about her dear mother, and a pang of home sickness pulled at her. She wanted to run to her loving arms and tell her what was happening to her. Her mother, she was sure, would find a way to nurture her and set things in their proper order. Jessica picked up the phone on an urge, and rang her parents home number in Boston. "Come on, Mom pick up the phone." Where could they be? Seven o'clock in Boston on a Friday evening, maybe, she thought, her father had taken her mother out for dinner. "I'll call later tonight." Not wanting to worry them, with her own problems, she decided she would wait until after her session with Dr. Hampton tomorrow.

She thought about the last conversation she had had with her parents. She had called them the day she had received the final divorce papers, which ended her three year marriage to Ken Moore. Her marriage had been a mistake, and she knew that they had never liked Ken.

Ken, Oh my, she said to herself. The first time she had met him she had been swept off her feet by the charming Mr. Ken Moore. There had been other guys in Boston but with her move to California for her new position with the Chronicle they had all been pushed aside. He still had a charm about him that was almost irresistible. An evening out with a few friends in a strange city had put her and Ken in the same surroundings on a clear spring night. A spring gala occasion filled with ambiance and romance had been the backdrop for their whirlwind marriage. Only after Ken had moved in and reality had set in did Jessica realize that Ken had hired a lawyer to do some research into her family and was very interested, especially with the finances, and the fortune of the Hatley estates. It just so happened the firm he had hired was an affiliate of Ash and Crawford. Ash and

Crawford had been her parents law firm for many years. The information had filtered back to the Boviers.

Her parents had warned her that her families name in Boston, would bring to her feet men looking for more than a dutiful wife. She had so hoped that by her move away from Boston, and to Long Beach, California, she could rid herself of all the criteria that followed the Hatleys and the Boviers. The prestigious Jo Anna Hatley Bovier, heiress of the Jefferson millions, that she had inherited from her mother, Rose Jefferson Hatley, was Jessica's mother.

She wanted to prove to herself she, Jessica Bovier, now Moore, could make a difference in this world on her own merit.

"Can I walk you out Jessica, or are you going to lock up?" Randal stuck his head inside her office. "Yes please, I would very much appreciate that," she said as she shut her computer off and picked up some notes she had been working on.

"That's it," she tried to sound nonchalant, but she wondered if Randal had been aware of the change in her. As they waited by the elevator she saw her reflection in a mirror over a small table. She had smoothed her long black hair into a French twist, and long wisps of hair fell over her cheekbones. She leaned forward, to look closer, and her dark brown eyes seemed to be even darker today. Was it for lack of sleep, she wondered?

The elevator ding sounded at the fifth floor. That was where the Chronicle employee's parked their cars.

"Thanks Randal." she said as he watched her get into her Jetta. She put the keys in the ignition and locked the door. She looked curiously around and waited for Randal to lead the way down the parking ramp. Then she went right to her apartment and walked quickly to the door and let herself in. Jessica had made a decision. She could hardly wait until tomorrow. A friend had told her about Dr. Hampton, and she was depending on him to clear her mind. Some very unusual things had been happening lately.

Jessica poured a Martini, ran the tub full of water and sat back and tried to put it all together. Now that she was safe here in her home, she wondered if she was being logical. "Oh well, what's it going to hurt to get Dr. Hampton's opinion," she reasoned.

Jessica struggled with sleeplessness and an ominous feeling of doom most of the night. The alarm clock rang at nine o'clock a.m. Her head was spinning and she tried to relieve some of the pressure with her fingers on her pulse zones. She focused on keeping herself occupied until her appointment at three o'clock. She spread the notebook full of papers on the table and forced herself to look at it. "This is not working," she slammed the papers back into her case. She wandered around doing odd jobs until it was time to leave.

Long Beach Doctor's Clinic, the sign was very clear. As she turned into the parking lot, Jessica wasn't sure what she would tell him. She took the elevator to the fourth floor. A sign pointed her to the right. She opened a door with Malcolm Hampton Phsc. clearly painted on the frosted window of the stained door.

A girl sat at the desk to the left. A man she assumed was the Doctor stood in front of it discussing something with her. He reached out his hand and she accepted it. "I'm Jessica Moore," she said.

"Come in and have a seat, we'll get right into your reason for coming, Jessica," Dr Hampton said as she followed him to his office. He turned and studied her while still moving things from off his desk. He paused for a second and then he pointed to a chair. He finally sat down in his black leather chair behind his desk. "This seems fine. Are you comfortable Miss Moore?" He pulled his glasses down on his nose, tapped his pen on his tablet, and really looked at her face for the first time since she had entered the room. "Now why don't you tell me what has been bothering you, Jessica you can start wherever you like." He was now ready to give her his attention.

"Dr. Hampton," she started. "I've always thought of myself as a very balanced person. I have a great job for the Long Beach Chronicle, a job I really had to work hard to get, and it's been really fulfilling for me. Well, well it seems like I've become paranoid. Things have been happening that are a bit unusual, and I feel as though I'm being stalked."

"Tell me why you feel threatened Jessica?" he once again tapped his pen and it made her nervous. "Do you have to do that?" she asked.

"What?" He held his pen up and looked at it. she shook her head. "Yes," he said. "So I can refer to it later."

Resigned, Jessica went on. "About a week ago a woman, came into my office. She asked my secretary if I was Jessica Moore from the Boston area?" My secretary came in and told me she was there. I stood up to greet her, and asked her her name.

'Donna,' she said, 'but I can't stay long.——I have a message for you.' She looked around, to be sure no one heard. I could tell she was anxious. She came around the desk, squeezed my arm, and pulled me closer, and spoke to me in a whisper." Jessica must have been staring into space, trying to recall exactly what had occurred, for Dr Campton's voice aroused her.

"Continue Jessica, what did she tell you?" he asked.

"She said, 'I have met someone who is a former acquaintance of yours, and I fear for your life. I have to warn you Miss Moore, please be careful.' Just then the phone rang. I picked it up and a mans voice said, 'this is Bob in the newsrooms. You need to come down here right away. There is a man here demanding to talk to you right now.' I excused myself and said I would be right back. When I got to the newsroom, no one was there, and no-one seemed to know who or where the man went. I hurried back to my office, but the woman, who had only identified herself as Donna was gone. I ran into the hall to see if I could find her, and I saw her at the elevator with a man. He had his arm through hers almost as if he was escorting her out. They were gone before I could reach them."

"Did you recognize him?" the Doctor asked.

"No not at all, I only saw him from the back. He seemed middle-aged, with graying hair, his back was slumped more than is normal." Jessica continued. "I seem to remember he wore some sort of hat."

"Did you ever see them again?" he asked.

"No, but there was something else. That evening when I got to my apartment, there was an unusual message on my answering machine. It was a woman's voice, I think I recognized it to be Donna. She sounded very nervous. She said, 'I'm sorry I had to leave Miss Moore. Please be very careful,' and then, as if someone had put a hand over her mouth she said 'Oh no,' and then a click.

"Now when did this take place?" he kept on writing.

"Lets see," she looked down at her watch, "this is June fifteenth, and so it was around June the eighth. I'd have the exact date marked on my appointment book if you need it." Jessica said.

"No, that won't be necessary. Is there anything else that you can remember that has been concerning you?" he asked.

"Only that I think someone is always watching me." she sighed.

"Can you be more specific?" his pen was still working its way across the paper.

"Yes, my office is on the tenth floor of the Namar Towers and I park in the sky-park. As I was leaving the elevator, and heading to my car, I saw a man parked about four cars away. I saw him watching me, but when I looked his way, he turned away," Jessica told him. "This happened to me twice within the last week."

"Okay, Miss Moore, what I would like you to do is keep a journal of the next weeks events. There are some specific things happening here, things that are not just in your mind. I would like to have you review some of your latest stories. Could it be someone is upset, because of a report you've released in the Chronicle? Think about it and make some notes for our next session." Dr. Hampton finally put his pen down, and Jessica surmised that their session was over. "Have you talked to anyone else about this?" he asked Jessica.

"No, should I go to the police.?" She had wondered if she should.

"Well, there's really nothing that couldn't have a logical explanation. So what could you go to the police with? Was anything missing from your office?"

"I didn't notice anything missing." Jessica already felt better having shared some of her doubts with Dr. Hampton.

They were through with the session and, Dr. Hampton rose and reached out his hand. Jessica extended hers and turned to the door. "Make an appointment with my secretary as you leave Jessica." he said as he handed her a card. "I've put my home number on the back, so call me if anything else upsets you. I'll see you next week sometime then."

Jessica's step was much lighter as she left the office. She sank into the seat of her Jetta, and headed to her favorite restaurant. She was hungry for the first time in weeks. It had just turned four thirty. The Italian restaurant had begun to flow with patrons for the after work happy hour. She ordered a martini. Jessica noticed Randal dining with a woman. She was very attractive in a showy sort of way. Not the type of woman she imagined Randal would become serious about. He noticed her and waved. She saw the woman look her way, displaying a flashy smile, she guessed he was explaining that they worked together. Tomorrow she would ask him where he found this one? Certainly not in a library. She chuckled to herself.

Ken and her used to frequent this restaurant. Sometimes Randal would bring a date and hang out with them. It hurt at times like this, Ken had been a good friend. It was only after their marriage that his rambling became noticeable. She expected all men to be like Adam, her father, devoted to one woman. She wondered if her mother appreciated the kind of husband she had. Jessica took her cell phone from her purse and rang the Hatley house once again. She let it ring six rings before she hung up. She shivered. She would try again when she got home. No news was better than bad news, and she certainly would hear if that were true, she decided. Jessica ate and satisfied herself, paid the waitress, and then she slipped out and headed to her apartment. The rain had subsided a little. She hoped she would sleep better tonight. She intended to put the thoughts of Donna, or what ever her name was, aside for now.

As Jessica unlocked her door she heard the phone ringing. She didn't reach it in time to stop the answering machine, so she sat down and listened. It was a mans voice.

"I am trying to reach Miss Jessica Moore. Jessica, this is your parent's lawyer in Boston. I'm afraid Miss Moore I have some tragic news for you. Please call me as soon as possible. Mr. Ash at——."

Jessica picked up the phone and rang her parents phone number. She was aware of the thumping of her heart. "More is wrong than is on the surface, something sinister." Jessica whispered. She opened the blinds and looked out at the rivulets of rain streaming down the window pane. The phone kept ringing, but there was no answer. Even if Jo Anna and Adam were occupied elsewhere, why weren't James and Mary, the butler and maid of Hatley House, answering. The situation seemed ominous.

Chapter Three

Jessica took a deep breath, her heart pounded and her face felt flushed. She realized there was three hours difference in time from California to Boston. She looked at her watch. California time was seven pm. So it would be ten pm. in Boston. Mr. Ash had listed a home number also. She wondered if Mr. Ash. would still be awake? Jessica steeled herself to what was ahead. Tragic! is what Mr. Ash had said. Trembling, she took a deep breath. Jessica picked up the phone, and made herself push the buttons. She dropped the receiver back in its place. "Relax, relax," she demanded her body, as she felt the pounding of her heart. She had a strange feeling that her life would change tonight. If her mother or father were okay they would have called her, Jessica reasoned.

She went to the bar and made a martini. She sat on the barstool and studied a picture of her mother Jo Anna, and her father, Adam Bovier, who had been completely devoted to her for so long a time. Once again her finger pressed the buttons on the phone. The rain riveting her patio window added to the insidious gloom that hung over her.

"Hello, this is the Ash residence," a man answered.

"Yes, this is Jessica Moore. Is this Mr. Ash?" she managed.

"Yes Miss Moore, you have the right number. I stayed up late, hoping you would call. Miss Moore, I think you need to make arrangements to come to Boston. your father needs you here.

"Is he okay? What has happened?" Jessica pleaded.

"There has been a shooting," his voice quivered. "Bare with me Jessica," he said. There was a pause, while he cleared his voice, and then Mr. Ash continued, "Jessica, there is no easy way to tell you this. Your mother is dead, she has been shot......It happened in the garden, at the Hatley Place. Jo Anna was already dead when the police got there......Your father heard the shot and he's the one that found them."

"Them? Where? Why? There must be a mistake." Jessica needed the facts. The reporter in her could not deal with reality without the facts.

"I'll tell you all I know, Jessica, but the police are still investigating. They have placed your father in custody pending the investigation. I am trying to arrange bail as we speak."

"My father, but why? He would never hurt my mother. I don't understand, why is he a suspect?'

"Joe, you know, Joe Santana, the gardener was found near Jo Anna. It seems he had tried to shield Jo Anna and was shot, Mr. Santana is dead as well.

"Mr. Ash, I will make arrangements to fly to Boston as soon as possible. Will you arrange it so I can see my Dad? I'll call you when I get there," Jessica said.

"Do you want me to make arrangements for a hotel?" he asked.

"No, of course not. I'll stay at my parents home." Jessica felt sick and a little impatient.

"Okay, but the police have not finished with their investigation," Mr. Ash wanted to shield her from the sight of the crime in the garden.

"Will you tell them I'll be there," Jessica could tell Mr. Ash was very shaken.

"Yes, I'll do whatever I can, both Jo Anna and Adam were my friends as well as my clients. Call me, and we'll get together when you get here. I am so sorry Jessica, this is not a phone call I was anticipating. Please accept my condolences."

Jessica laid the phone in the cradle, and she opened the French doors and walked onto the patio. The rain had stopped and the air was clean after the rain. She breathed in sharply and some of the fever left her body. She sipped the damp air like dry wine. Her life had been completely smashed, but she felt nothing.

Like a deep wound the pain was still ahead. She sat there numb for some time, and then she remembered her drink at the bar. Jo Anna's picture caught her eye. She clasped it to her chest and she made it to her bedroom before she fell apart. Jessica sobbed herself to sleep and was awakened by the ringing of the phone. She managed to reach it on the bed-stand.

"Jessica, this is Randal Scott. Are you coming into the office this morning? There's some work the boss wants edited today for this evening paper."

"O! Randal, I've had a crisis in my family. I need to fly to Boston as soon as I can make arrangements. Will you fill in for me? I can't tell you how long I'll be gone. There's been a death," her voice cracked. "My mother is dead," Jessica spared herself the pain of repeating all she knew.

"I am so sorry Jessica. I understand, your place is with your family now. I'll tell the boss, and let us know what we can do," Randal said.

"Thanks, and will you tell my secretary to arrange a flight to Boston for me. Ask her to give me a call when it's arranged," Jessica was wide awake now.

"I will do it, and you fly safe, and come back soon. We will all miss you." Randal had been a real friend. He was there for her when she went through a divorce from Ken Moore.

Jessica felt pensive and subdued this morning. There was no time for salving over her emotional scars today, she would need every ounce of strength she could muster to deal with what awaited her in Boston.

Flight arrangements were made, and Melanie, Jessica's secretary, called to tell her where she would find her tickets. As she locked the door of her apartment, Jessica wondered how long she would be gone, or if she would even come back to California. Would anything ever be the same? Even though Jo Anna was gone, how would she ever still her voice. Hatley House was where Jo Anna was raised by her parents Rose and John Hatley, who had adopted her as an infant. How would Adam ever get over this? And yet she knew they all would, just as Jo Anna had survived without her mother, Rose. But oh, how hard it was when it was your turn. Death was so un-amendable. Tears fought her eye lids and fell down her cheeks.

She found the tickets exactly where Melanie said. "Gate thirty, Miss Moore and we have a airbus ready to escort you to your aircraft," the agent said.

"Thank you," she said as she handed the airbus driver a tip.

She picked up a Long Beach Chronical, paid the lady, and slipped it into her briefcase and headed down the boarding ramp. Jessica noticed a man coming down the ramp waving at her. It couldn't be him, she thought. He was making his way toward her smiling. He took her in his arms, and tears fell down her face. He reached into his pocket for a handkerchief and gently wiped her cheek.

"I'm sorry darling, I didn't mean to make you cry. Am I that ugly?"

"I didn't mean to cry on you, Ken. It's just a bad time for me," Jessica explained. Ken's familiar arms felt so good. He held her for a minute, and she let him, and then they were moved ahead by the crowd. Jessica had found her seat in first class, but had lost track of Ken until the flight attendant was closing the aircraft door, and they were told to prepare for take-off. It was then that she saw Ken again. He was busy talking to an attendant. She escorted him to the seat next to Jessica.

"Have a good flight Mr. Moore. Can I get you two a drink?"

"Two martini's will do nicely, thank you miss." Ken was still a man in charge she observed, but she was glad to have him there.

After another martini they ate, and then the lights were lowered. Ken reached over and took her hand. Jessica remembered how persuasive he could be. Their relationship had been of a tenuous sort. She had to remind herself that they were divorced. Ken was not a one-woman man, but right now she needed him. So she looked in his eyes and they talked. She shared with him all that was going on in her life.

He listened and then he put his arms around her and he said, "Go to sleep honey, you'll need your energy tomorrow."

Jessica slept until they were asked to buckle their seatbelts for landing in Chicago. This was Ken's destination. Once on the ground, Ken prepared to leave.

"I wish you the best Jessica," he said. "Let's keep in touch." Gently he took her face in his hands and kissed her ever so softly on the lips, and he touched her lips with his finger as if he was remembering, and then he drew away. He looked back and waved as the crowd pushed him out of the plane and down the ramp.

"Ken, Ken, wait," Jessica called to him, as he disappeared, she realized how she had missed him, and she felt so alone. She jumped out of her seat and pushed her way through the crowd, and ran down the ramp. She stopped to catch her breath when she finally reached the terminal. Then she watched as he greeted a very attractive woman. Jessica sighed as Ken hugged the woman and than he tucked his arm in hers and walked out of Jessica's life once again.

She would do well to remind herself why they were divorced. Ken was a womanizer, a flirt, and flirting was a game that disrupted marriages. It was said to be like a diluting of the fine wine of marriage with water. It was a game to build the ego of those with low self-esteem. Theirs had been diluted many times.

Jessica thought about her father. He had been a loyal husband to Jo Anna. Adam had been a good example to all married men. How could anyone think he could hurt Jo Anna in any way. Jessica would have bet her life on that.

The boarding call to Boston got her attention. Jessica took her briefcase from the overhead and put it on the seat next to her. She hoped no-one would need the seat. The flight attendants made their round for snacks and drinks. "Not this time," she refused the martini she was offered. No more martinis and no more men. That mixture is dangerous she decided. She could become formidable if she was so inclined, and from now on she was determined to be just that.

Jessica opened her briefcase and found the Chronicle. On the front page was an enlarged picture of a woman on a cot, being carried to an ambulance. Her face was uncovered for a reason. The Police were asking for identification. She was found drowned in a local lake. Possibly the lake near Namar Towers, she could see from her office window, she thought. There was reason to believe she had been the victim of foul play, the article read. The body could have been there no more than four days,' the article continued. "That's her," Jessica gasped so loud, she caught the attendants attention.

There was no doubt, the picture was of Donna, the woman who had came to her office to warn her to be careful. Jessica wondered about the man she had seen with her at the elevator. Was the call she got from the newsroom a decoy, to keep Donna from talking to her? Had the man at the elevator caused Donna's death?

"Is everything okay Mrs. Moore?" the attendant asked.

"I don't know how it could be any worse." Jessica drew a deep breath and let it out slowly.

The pretty blond attendant, reached down and touched Jessica's arm, "Mr. Moore told me that you had lost your mother. I'm sorry Mrs. Moore."

"When did he tell you that? Jessica asked.

"Just before the flight out of Long Beach. That's why I switched him with another passenger. He said he would like to sit with his wife, since you had just got news of your mother's death. He's not continuing the flight with you I take it."

"No he's not, he had another engagement in Chicago," Jessica retorted.

"Oh, I see. Well if there is any thing I can do for you let me know." she smiled and went on with her work.

"Sooo!" she sighed. "He knew before he got on the flight." Jessica had been so busy talking about herself, that she never did ask him what he was doing in California. She wondered now, if Ken knew this woman, whose picture was in the news.

What was it Donna had said? 'She had met an old acquaintance, and she was scared for me.' Now Donna was dead. If only she would have asked. Who?

Who could she trust? Was Ken the old acquaintance? If not, then who? Jessica wondered. As she put the paper back in her suitcase she felt the paranoia consuming her again. Jessica wondered if something stronger than malice was operating against her. But why? She couldn't think of any reason. As soon as she arrived at Hatley Place she would call Dr. Hampton.

As soon as the lights were lowered, Jessica stared out of the aircraft window. Overhead ragged clouds appeared showing through patches of gray. She asked for a blanket, pulled it around her, and tried not to think for the rest of the flight.

Chapter Four

Jessica watched the red ball rise slowly above the horizon from the aircraft window. As they circled the capital city of Massachusetts, Boston Bay lay just beneath them, at the mouth of the Charles River.

The Captain spoke from the cockpit. "We are waiting Ladies and Gentlemen for a landing slot to open," he said. "Probably no more than five minutes and we'll have you on the ground at Logan International Airport. Thank you for flying with us and have a great day."

Logan Airport was always crowded, mostly due to the health care facilities, including many teaching hospitals and many institutions that pioneer in medical research. Boston was also the home of high technology industries, computer, electronic, and engineering firms that created employment throughout the city. Jessica remembered an essay she had wrote about the Boston

Harbor. The city of Boston was located on a magnificent natural harbor opening to the Massachusetts Bay. At one time the city occupied a relatively narrow piece of land. This restricted city expansion. The tidal flats were filled extensively and that had added to the city.

Once on the ground and inside Logan Airport, Jessica tried once again to call the Hatley House. James and Mary Morgan, the butler and cook, were not answering the phone. Where were they? she wondered. She was anxious to see her father, and would do so as soon as possible.

A uniformed driver appeared at the gate. He held a sign. Jessica Moore was written in big print. "So," she said. "I have been taken care of after all."

"Yes, Mr. Ash asked me to meet you, Miss Moore." the driver took her bags and soon they were headed out of Logan Airport and west on the Massachusetts's turnpike. "I am so sorry about your mother, Miss Hatley. She will be greatly missed by many. She was one of the great ladies of our era," he volunteered as we exited the turnpike. They passed by the Shaw monument and the State house. Many tourists were visible as they passed the Freedom Trail, a self guided walkway tour that connected the city with other historic sites.

The excitement of her home-coming to Boston was lessened in light of Jo Anna's death, and the realization that her mother would never enjoy her dearly loved Boston again. Jessica tried to shift her focus on her immediate concern, her father.

"We're here," the driver announced as they turned onto Hatley Avenue and then into the drive. The giant brass gates, attached to the brick pillars swung opened when Jessica summoned them with her code card. No one was to be seen, as she tipped the driver. The three story, rosewood brick mansion, with beautifully carved, dark green shutters, had stood over one hundred and fifty years. Jefferson Estates had been upgraded when Rose Hatley had inherited it after the early death of Rose's parents in an automobile accident. At that time it had been renamed The Hatley House. The house stood but the owners did not. If only this house could talk, it would most certainly have a story to tell. Tears filled Jessica's eyes as she turned the key and opened the doors to Hatley Place and walked into silence. The similarity was to that of a great mausoleum, being visited by those mourning.

The great hall and entry area were as she remembered, open and expanding three stories. From the center of the room an elaborate crystal chandelier hung. The circular stair cases flowed from two sides of the great hall, that led to the rooms on the second and third floors. Circular half-walls began where the stairs ended to form a half moon. Ivy hung from each balcony, leaving a floral effect.

On the main floor, large mahogany double doors led to the library to the left and to the dining area to the right. At the center of the room stood a Georgia stone fireplace that extended all three floors and to the ceiling. Three huge slabs of white marble formed mantles that served as a base from which English ivy hung, and upon which beautiful oriental vases sat. On each side of the fireplace were mahogany French doors that led to the family living room. A large room that her grandmother Rose, had decorated originally, but now filled with touches that her mother had so painstakingly furnished. Tall dark bookcases had been built into the walls, filled with special effects of knick-knacks and collectables. The carpet was a rich oriental. Grand mahogany pieces of furniture in vividly printed colors filled the room. In front of the fireplace set smartly arranged settees.

Sliding glass doors extended even further to the patio and oblong pool. Shrubs of various colors and shapes adorned the area. Beyond were more gardens and paths that led to unique outdoor rooms, covered with arches of ivy or roses, each having it's own theme. Joe Santana had cared for these gardens for many years in the service of Jo Anna and Adam Bovier. Even before that he had worked for her grandparents Rose and John Hatley.

Jessica heard voices. She walked through the grand entry, into the living room and stood staring out of the French doors, as two men dressed as policemen surrounded a particular spot they seemed to be concerned with. She turned away, she wasn't ready to view that ominous scene. She had to sit down before her knees buckled. She collapsed on a chair in front of the television, and flipped the remote to the local news channel.

"The death of Jefferson heiress, Mrs. Jo Anna Hatley Bovier is still a mystery. It is still being investigated further by police officers. Her husband Adam Bovier is being held without benefit of bond. No formal charge has been made against him at the moment," the anchorman blared loudly.

She could not listen. Jessica hit the remote to off, and forced herself to focus. Her face showed bewilderment. She bent forward, and covered her face with her hands. What she needed was a plan, and right now she didn't know where to start. She pulled her bags into the elevator, picked up her briefcase, and pushed three. Her old room had not been changed since her move to Long Beach. That was where she would stay for now, until this mystery was solved and her beloved father, Adam Bovier, was home where he belonged.

Jessica had opened her bags, hung her dresses, pulled back the sheets, and stepped into the shower, when the phone rang. She turned off the water and listened.

"Miss Moore, this is Mr. Ash. I hope you had a good flight. I would like to see you in my office tomorrow morning. I'll have a car pick you up at nine am."

"Not even death can stop time for the living. Nothing stands still, we go ahead or we go back, and Jessica had to muster strength to go ahead." She pulled on a robe, unlocked the door and walked out onto the balcony. She looked toward the gardens. The pool was dark as well as the area marked with yellow ribbon. The paths that ran through the gardens beamed with dim sparkling lights. The voices she had heard earlier were gone. The cottage that had been Joe Santana's, was lit up. Jessica could see movement on the porch. Joe Santana's family had came in from Mexico, Jessica surmised.

Moonlight fell dappled through the clouds. The night voices spoke of things she recognized, and did not fear. The chirping of small creatures, the breeze in the trees, and a voice of silence, that reached clear to the stars.

She locked the doors and pulled open the drapes and let the moonlight play on her walls. She sat on her bed, exhausted. She crossed her arms and rocked from side to side. The earth seemed to tilt, and she had all she could do to keep her balance. Finally she knelt by the side of her bed, and prayed for her father, and for the strength she needed to face tomorrow. When her feet left the floor, and her body was horizontal, exhaustion took over.

Outside the neon lights flashed above the La Qinta sign. He sat in the well used chair and snatched at his ear, a habit from his youth. It had irritated his mother when he rubbed it until it bled. It was starting to bleed. His plan hadn't went the way he wanted it to. What was it his mother always said. There is always a catch in the best laid plans of men and mice.

He had found Jessica. His sister was beautiful. Her long black hair, and olive skin, she looked a lot like Jo Anna he thought. He had watched Jo Anna die, crumple to the ground. Joe Santana had tried to protect her for you, Adam. Now he's gone too. I hated her. My mother hated her. Why did you do it Adam? Why did you get my mother pregnant and then desert us?

Donna, the little doe, she always liked it when I called her that. She wouldn't listen to me. Why, oh why Donna, he missed her. His pills were running out. He'd have to figure out a way to get some. He dropped his head and started sobbing. Mama, Donna, why does everyone always leave me. You'll pay Adam.

Chapter Five

The blue and magenta clouds cast misty hues that floated up and down Jessica's wall. It was dajavu. Clouds had played games here with her before. She closed her eyes again, and thought of her family, and what had happened to them, until a brilliant blaze of sunlight allowed to her lounge no longer.

Dressed and ready for her appointment, she wandered through the house. She opened the double doors and walked to the front gates. She gathered the mail and took it into the library. As she flipped through the letters she noticed a card from James and Mary.

"From the Bahamas with love. Be home soon." That was why they hadn't answered the phone, when she had called. It was not in their character to just up and leave Hatley House unattended. There was more to this then was on the surface, but the answer would have to come later. She would ask her father when she was allowed to visit him.

That was when Jessica realized that James and Mary didn't know about her mother, and Joe Santana. How would they know? They were gone before that day.

She laid the card down on the desk, and let her hand rub the surface. There was some memory there but her mind couldn't tell her what her senses remembered. Was she with Jo Anna when she bought this Queen Anne desk with the brass handles? She gazed at the reflection in the mirror above the desk. The reflection resembled Jo Anna, but she was quite sure the mirror knew the difference.

Once again she was drawn to the window looking toward the gardens. The men in uniform were back. She looked beyond them to the cottage and the shed that stood next to it. That was where Mr. Santana had lived and worked. She wondered if something that happened long ago was connected to what was happening now. A horn beeped, but she ignored it. Her thoughts were of her Grandmother Rose.

Rose was tall and thin boned, with soft white hair, always graciously styled, but not extreme. John Hatley, her husband, seemed to tower over her, unless Rose had on high-heels. Jessica thought of the time when she was about ten years old, she had knocked on the door of their rooms.

"Come in," her grandfather had said. He stood behind her grandmother, who was seated at her vanity, brushing her hair. It hung to her waist, and it was the only time she had ever seen it down. "Here you take over," her grandfather winked at her. Jessica thought it was the most beautiful hair she had ever seen, like pure white gold. Jo Anna's had been of a coarser and thicker texture, and was black.

Her grandfather called down for some hot chocolate and sweet cakes. They were placed on the table in front of the fireplace. Jessica curled up to her grand-mother on the settee, and her grandfather sat in his rocker. The three of them had talked until late in the night. It was on that night that she learned her grandparents were well to do. Rose had inherited the Jefferson billions from her parents and someday, Jessica might be responsible for the Hatley Estates. When it had gotten late they had both walked with her to her bedroom, kissed her goodnight, and tucked her in bed. Such memories were precious. They remained in the recesses of the mind, to be pulled up, when there was nothing physical to hold on to.

Jessica jumped as someone touched her arm. Surprised she turned to find a shockingly handsome man standing there.

"Miss. Moore, there is a cab out front, the driver said he was here to pick you up."

"Oh yes, thank you." She reached out to shake his hand, well aware of his towering presence, and aware that he had just touched her arm ever so gently.

"I'm so sorry, Miss Moore, I didn't mean to startle you. You seemed a million miles away. I'm Al Torres, and I know you are Jessica. If you would like me to send the cab away, I will use the limo to take you where ever you need to go."

"Thank you, Mr. Torres, I would appreciate that.," she said, once more in control. I feel like I should recognize you," Jessica said.

"I live in Spain with my family," he said. "I'm a guest in the gardener's cottage. I'm doing a few things around the place to show my appreciation." Al quickly turned away and walked toward the garages.

Mr. Torres opened the limo door for Jessica. He reached for her arm, and supported her, she was aware of his dark eyes probing hers deeper than she wanted him to. It left her feeling uneasy.

The Imperial building was familiar to Jessica. She had been here with her parents. They had insisted that she be with them when they had their wills made. As their only child Jessica stood to inherit what was theirs, upon their deaths. Except for a stepbrother, Adam's son by his first marriage, she was it. Jessica had never seen him since he lived out of the country with his mother. Later he had been put in an institution, and was not able to care for himself.

She arrived early, so she sat in Mr. Ash's waiting room and opened her briefcase. She looked briefly at the front page of the Chronical, at the picture of Donna, and then filed it in back of her other papers. "That would have to wait," she thought.

"The funeral has been arranged, with your approval, of course." Mr. Ash offered. "Jo Anna had been a part of several women's auxiliary societies. They all wanted to help and it is all being organized by my secretary, as we speak. What do you think about the Old North Church?" He was trying to cover the immediate problems. "Of course, Jo Anna will be buried in the Jefferson cemetery near her mother and father Rose and John Hatley," Mr. Ash looked up at her finally. "That was her request, Jessica," he said, as though she might question him.

"What I want to know is not so much about the funeral, Mr. Ash. I want to know if my father will be there? I want to know when I can see him? We've both lost someone we love very much. Don't you understand? Mr. Ash I need my father," Jessica was upset, and she held her head and wiped away the tears.

"I do understand Miss Moore, and since I talked to you in Long Beach, I've started an investigation of my own. I think when you are ready, we'll sit down and go over the facts." Mr. Ash went to the door and asked his secretary to get her a glass of water and tissues. When he was seated, Jessica continued.

"They are saying that my father killed my mother out of jealousy, and that Mr. Santana was shot trying to protect her. Those are not facts, Mr. Ash, those are speculations. What proof do they have?" Jessica was releasing all the feelings she had contained for the last three days. "Now where, Mr. Ash, where are the facts?"

Mr. Ash's secretary knocked lightly, and set a glass of water on the desk, and handed Jessica a box of tissues. Jessica could sense another presence, but she was waiting for the answer.

"The facts are Miss. Moore, They do have a gun, the Count's gun, and it does have his fingerprints on it. So far the only motive they have, and are trying to prove, is a crime of passion." "So Miss Moore, They consider your father guilty until proven different." Mr. Ash excused himself and walked out and left the door open. Jessica wondered if Mr. John Ash was hiding something. She didn't quite trust him. His demeanor depicted a deep resentment toward her father. She was surprised since she thought of them as old friends, college buddies.

Al Torres watched Mr. Ash leave, before he knocked lightly. Jessica stood up as he entered. He took her hand in his, and touched it to his face, and she felt the empathy he had for her. "I'm so sorry Jessica, I wish there was something I could do." He reached out to support her. When she had gained her composure, she moved back and looked at him. "I thought you had left, Mr. Torres." she said.

"I had an errand, and decided to slip back and see if you were through for the day." he said. When they reached the elevator, he cupped her chin with his hand, looked her tenderly and whispered. "Do you think you could call me Al and I could call you Jessica," He put his arm around her shoulder and looked her in the eyes. The ding, ding of the elevator, brought her back to reality, or was it something else. Something lodged in the recesses of her mind, something of the betrayal she had known with Ken. She would not trust him fully as a friend. They walked silently to the limo.

As they drove through the narrow streets, crowded with gabled houses, built wall against wall, Jessica was once again lacerated by pain. Pain goaded by old memories.

Jessica looked at the man driving. His head was of a manly shape. His thick hair was blue black, with a glossy look of health. His eyes were as dark as his hair. His skin not yet weathered, as Joe Santana's had been after years of garden work. She could however see a resemblance. Were Joe and Al Torres related? But how? Jessica wondered.

John Ash wasn't happy with himself. If he was going to pull this off he would have to show less of his resentment toward Jessica. He knew she was due to inherit a large sum of money from Jo Anna, and this stuck in his craw. It was he that The Count Adam Bovier had depended on to care for all his business. Not Jessica. It's true, he had been paid well all these years. But it was a pittance of what he deserved. Loyalty, pooey, he thought. It was the fringe benefits that kept him tied to The Count and Countess Bovier.

John was parked in front of the prison, but before he went in to visit Adam he had a little work to do. He pulled a brief case from under the car-seat and pulled out two papers and an envelope. The envelope had been addressed to him, John Ash

Attorney at Law, in behalf of Adam Bovier. The letter was demanding money, much more money than the last time. Adam had already paid ten thousand dollars to assure Jessica's safety. This time {one million dollars} was to be the ransom price. The kind of payment, cash, and the drop-off spot was included. "How much is your daughter worth?" It was signed, Guess Who? John hesitated, and then he slipped the copy into the envelope. Now, John was ready to visit his client, and old dear friend in his time of calamity. He hoped Adam was feeling very protective of his beloved Jessica today.

Chapter Six

Al drove directly to the Hatley House. Several times she caught him as he studied her face intently. She had used his arms as a refuge, just as she had used Kens, Jessica told herself. She was in control now, so when he opened the car door, she thanked him and shook his hand. He took the key from her hand and noticed a newspaper near his feet. He bent down and picked up the Boston Globe. When Jessica reached for it, he held it tightly. He smiled jokingly, and then he leaned over and kissed her on the cheek. Once again Jessica caught him as he studied her face.

"What? Do I have lipstick on my tooth? she asked.

"No!" he laughed. "You remind me of someone I know, you could pass for sisters."

Before she could ask, he got into the limo and was gone. As she stood there she wondered who she reminded him of. Out of the corner of her eye, she watched as a black suburban slowly cruised past the double gates. Jessica shivered.

She locked the door as she stepped in, slipped out of her heels, and walked to the library. She set her briefcase on the sideboard, and opened the newspaper.

'THE COUNTESS Jo Anna Hatley Bovier...One of Boston's great Ladies.'

The Boston Globe had dedicated a two page section to Jessica's mother. The front page was a enlarged picture of The Countess Jo Anna Bovier, a picture taken at one of Boston's regal occasions.

Who were Jo Anna's parents? Were they aware of her death, even though they had given her up years ago? These were questions that may need to be answered if she were to help her father now. Finally, would they be considered Jo Anna's next of kin if Jessica were gone? Where would this end? Pretty scary, she thought.

Jessica studied her mothers face in detail. Jo Anna had long dark hair and brown eyes. She let her finger run over her high cheekbones, and her thin delicate frame. Jessica looked into the mirror above the table. A resemblance of her mother looked back at her. She had never been curious about her heritage until then. She wondered if the past might be tied somehow to the present. If she had a another grandmother out there somewhere, she certainly would like to know.

Jessica continued reading. 'Rose and John Hatley had adopted a baby girl, who turned out to be 'The Countess Jo Anna Hatley Bovier' heiress to the Jefferson billions. Jessica leafed through the special section, she noticed on several occasions Jo Anna was standing with or near Joe Santana. The Botanical Society had sponsored these dinners. What really held Jessica's curiosity was the obvious love that radiated from Joe Santana eyes as he looked at her mother. "Was it true then? Was he infatuated with her mother? Was her father jealous?" She had never witnessed such vibrations in them.

Jessica picked up the phone and rang Mr. Ash's number. "Mr. Ash, when can I see my father?" Jessica left a message. He would know who it was, she thought, if only from the frustration in her voice. Or was it distrust?

Tears filled her eyes, as she walked to the French doors that lead to the pool and looked out. No sign of policemen today. The yellow ribbons were gone. Did that mean they had made a decision? Jessica would like to know.

Jessica hoped someday she would be able to enjoy the pool and the gardens. Perhaps the hurt would pass, as all things pass with the healing of years. She saw some movement by the cottage, but she couldn't make out what was going on. Mr. Ash had given Joe Santana's family permission to stay there until a new gardener could be hired. His family were flying in from Mexico. How did Al Torres fit into this family, she was curious?

Jessica decided to use this time to make some phone calls. She would do that from her room. She closed her door, sat on the bed, and started down her list. She started with the Chronical in California.

"Take your time Jessica," her boss had assured her that her job was intact.

"Can I talk to Randal?" she asked.

"Hi, Jessica are you holding in there?" he asked.

"I'm okay I guess," she said. "Randal, I'm curious about the woman who had drowned several days before I left Long Beach? Was she ever identified?"

"Her name was Donna Mavis. It seems that she had just been released from a mental hospital in upper New York. Her husband and two year old daughter were killed in a car accident while Donna was driving. She had tried to commit suicide at that time, and may have accomplished it this time. On the other hand," Randal explained, "she had traveled to California with a male companion, so the police have not made a final ruling. They are still hunting the man. Anyway, no next of kin was located, so she was buried by the State of New York."

Jessica wondered about Donna Mavis. She seemed like a sweet lady. Jessica wished she would have spent more time with her. Who was it she had tried to warn her about? Would she ever know? Could she have prevented the drowning? Jessica couldn't see how. It still tormented her when she thought of the picture of Donna in the globe.

"Will you send me the latest copies that have reference to her case?" Jessica asked him.

"I'll be glad to." Randal said.

He was curious about things in Boston, so she filled him in.

"Are congratulations in order?" She teased him about the girl she had seen him with. He just laughed. "That's what I thought," she said, and then they said goodbye and hung up.

The next call was to Mr. Hampton's office. His secretary put her right through to the doctor. Jessica filled him in, and listened to his condolences.

Jessica picked up the pile of important papers she had found in the library. She propped herself up on her pillow and began to sort through them. Any information about her mothers adoption might lead to someone who might be willing to kill for her mothers money.

Could Ken be put in that category? Ken gambled, in more ways than one, and had some major debts, due to a paternity suit he was fighting in court. He was a womanizer, but a killer? she doubted that. Although, he was a private detective, could he have learned something about Jo Anna's real parents and tried to blackmail Jo Anna and John? Jessica felt guilty for her thoughts. "After all Ken was still her friend wasn't he?" she shook her head. At the present friend or foe had no face.

As she sorted, a family tree caught her attention. It was more like a page in an old scrap book. The book had pictures as well as old newspaper articles. She hoped it would include something about her mothers adoption. 'Rose Jefferson had married John J. Hatley. They had no children of their own. They decided to adopt. Their adopted little girl was Jo Anna Hatley, {Jessica's mother}.'

"My mother the Belle of Boston," Jessica smiled as she looked at the many photos taken at the gala occasions shown in the clippings she had sorted through. One of the gossip columns caught her eye.

'Count Adam Bovier has won the hand of Miss Jo Anna Hatley in marriage, in spite of his scandalous divorce. It seemed as if The Count's ex-wife, Dorothy, had won in court one half of Adams money as well as custody of their five year old son, Lawrence, and had left the country.' The article featured a picture of a woman and a small boy, leaving the courthouse. Microphones were shoved in her face, and she was making a statement. The article stated.

'I only got what I deserved, after all I did have his child.' She was dressed in a very modest dress, with her light blond hair trimmed neatly at shoulder length.

There was more to this woman than superficial veneer, Jessica discerned, she was dressed for the part. The loving wife and mother, deserted by the wealthy husband. Jessica felt nothing but pity for the woman in the picture.

Jessica laid the paper back on the table. She had heard about Adam's son Lawrence, but only briefly. She had once asked her father where he was, and her father had said, 'He is where he belongs.'

That meant that Jessica might have a brother out there somewhere, if he was still alive. She would ask her father tomorrow. She hoped her father would be out of the prison in time to come to Jo Anna's funeral. Jessica yawned and pulled her pillow out from under the bedspread, sunk into it and slept.

The phone rang and woke her. She rubbed her eyes. Jessica surmised that she had slept for hours. A sunset of amethyst and crimson streaked across the western skyline. She jumped up and reached for the phone, but it stopped ringing. She picked it up and carried it to the door. She heard a click as a door shut, and then she heard footsteps on the balcony. With her ear to the door, she heard footsteps going down the stairs. Jessica dialed 911, and opened the door. She ran to the stairs and was half way down to the second level when she heard the click of the kitchen door as it closed. She shook as she sat on the top step of the staircase.

"Hello, did you call 911?" she heard a voice, and raised the phone to her ear.

"Yes," Jessica replied. "There was someone in my house, but whoever it was is gone now." Jessica hung up. She took the elevator to the first floor, walked to the kitchen, and checked the door. It was locked. She sat on a stool by the counter, she squeezed the telephone tightly to her chest before the tears started. "Someone had a key to her house, but who? How? And more importantly why?"

Jessica jumped when the phone rang again. "Hi sweetheart, guess who?" a very familiar voice crooned across the line.

"Ken, where are you?" she cried.

"I'm in town doll, and I can be at your side in fifteen minutes. Better yet make it twenty five minutes and be dressed to dine with an old friend. You can tell me all about it then." Ken hung up the phone before she could refuse.

Where had Ken been just minutes before? Jessica asked herself. She would find out what he was up to tonight. There were other things she needed to talk to him about, such as, did he know Donna Mavis? And who was the woman he had met in Chicago?

Jessica heard the door chime, and she let Ken in. She let him give her a hug and then excused herself and went to get a wrap. She remembered a silk scarf of her mothers that would go with her dress.

She opened the door to her mother's room. She turned on the light and stood transfixed. Someone had been there. The room was a mess with strewn possessions. Jo Anna's drawers had been dumped and scattered. A portrait of Jo Anna had been pulled from where it hung on the wall. It had been slashed with a sharp object and thrown to the floor. This was deliberate. There was ugly purpose here. Jessica screamed, and then fell to the floor.

She awoke to the sound of voices coming from the great hall. She was on the couch in the living room and she felt strong gentle hands touching her face. Jessica had felt these hands before and she knew without opening her eyes who they belonged to.

"Where's Ken?" she asked. The last she remembered was Ken standing at the front door. Now Al moved away and stood at the end of the couch.

"He's with a detective, Jessica, they are going to interview you as soon as you feel up to it. I'm glad to see you are okay. I'm going to go to the kitchen and make you some hot tea. I'll tell them you're awake." This time Al avoided her eyes.

Jessica wondered what story Ken had told him? She was still sputtering to herself when Ken and another man walked in. "You're a detective?" she asked. "Are you off duty?"

"She's better," Ken grinned at her and winked at the other man. "This is Scott Smith, Jessica," Ken introduced him to her. "He's a private investigator. He works for our detective agency, and is working on the Hatley case. He's going to ask you a few questions."

Scott Smith was what she called a hunk. Jessica wondered what gym he frequented. He had a crew cut, and was clean shaven. The kind of guy everyone wanted on their team. When he sat beside her she was aware of how nice he smelled. He smiled at her warmly.

"Was someone in your house today?" he questioned Jessica.

"Yes," she said, "just before Ken called. I was sleeping and the phone rang. I heard footsteps in the hall and then I heard someone run down the steps. Who ever it was used the kitchen door."

"Who has a key?" he continued.

"Only my father and mother, and me. Oh! and James and Mary, the butler and his wife. They work for my parents. They are on vacation right now, and should be back in a few days," she hoped.

"Can you think of anything someone would break in to get?" Scott asked.

"Were they after her jewelry? I can't think of anything else," Jessica said. "Or could it have something to do with Jo Anna and Joe's murder?"

"I'm afraid I can't answer that yet. I suggest on the other hand that you be very careful. It is my job to know where you are at all times. Okay, so here is a card with my number, keep it with you, and if you need me I will be close by. Oh, if you can think of anyone else with a key let me know." Scott shook her hand and he and Ken walked out together.

Al had found a tray and had fixed her some tea. She noticed he had brought two cups so she cleared the coffee table for him and they sat opposite each other in silence. They didn't need to talk, Jessica could tell by his expression that he was concerned, but also deeply troubled.

Finally Al spoke. "I took a message for you Jessica, it was from Mr. Ash. Be at his office at ten a.m. if you would like to see your father." Al stood up and started toward the door and without looking back he said, "your husband said he would be here to take care of you. Goodnight Jessica."

Ken let Scott and Al out, locked the door and came into the living room, and stretched out on the couch.

"What do you think you are doing?" Jessica demanded.

"I'm staying, I'll sleep here in the living room," Ken insisted.

"Goodnight then," she said, and she picked up her shoes, walked to the elevator, pushed three, and went up to her room, and locked the door.

Jessica was relieved Ken had stayed. Even though she wasn't sure of his game plan, she thought she would sleep better tonight. She couldn't get to sleep though. She finally put on her robe and went out on the balcony. She sat on the wicker lounge, and pulled her knees up and hugged them.

What was Al hiding? She realized something deeply troubled him. More than just grieving for Joe Santana. She would try to talk to him again tomorrow.

Jessica viewed the gardens. The ground level lanterns threw shadows on the trees. The night sky sparkled with stars.

Meo Rose

They only served as reminders of her father. Oh, how badly Jessica wanted to see him at home.

Beyond the cottage was still lit up, and she wondered if Al was sitting on the porch looking at the luminous sky and hearing the night sounds? Was she imagining it or had he sounded betrayed when he mentioned Ken staying to take care of her? What had Ken told him? She hoped Al could see through Ken's purpose.

Once again worry for her father overtook any thoughts of her own personal happiness. A sense of isolation overcame her. Who was in the garden that night? What had he wanted? What stopped Adam from shooting Jo Anna's murderer? She thought her father knew the answers. Why, oh why wouldn't he tell her?

Jessica locked the glass door behind her and pulled the shades. She went back to the pile of papers and sorted some more. A clip of pictures caught her attention. Adam, a woman and a child about four years old, were standing by a big tree, in front of a big house. She flipped it over. Adam with Dorothy and Laurence it read.

Chapter Seven

The phone was ringing when Jessica stepped out of the shower. Ken answered it in the kitchen. "Jessica, you have a call. It's the Morgans, James and Mary." he called to her on the intercom. Jessica picked up the receiver in her room.

"Hello Jessica," Mary began, "we just got into Miami. We are at the airport and we are watching the news. We can't believe what we are hearing. Tell us it's not true."

Jessica, felt relieved just to hear Mary's voice. "It is true, Mary, isn't it terrible. I'm so sorry you had to hear about it that way. When will you be here? The house is so empty without you and James, and Adam, and Jo Anna."

Jessica how is your father?" when Jessica didn't say anything, she went on. "We'll be home tomorrow."

"Good," Jessica choked. "Mother's funeral is tomorrow at two p.m. She would want you to be there—," she couldn't continue. She hit the intercom and said, "Ken will you fill them in?" she heard the click on the other end.

Jessica went to the vanity and splashed water over her face. It seemed that in her whole life, everything had rotated around Jo Anna. "She's gone, and I'm here. Can I ever become the blazing sun that she had been. There to brighten the moon and the universe around her?" she spoke to Jo Anna's likeness in the mirror.——

When Jessica went into the kitchen Ken was already there. He had made ham and cheese omelet's and was toasting bread. Two places were set on the table. He swooped to her side and pecked her on the cheek, at the same time he pulled the chair out for her to be seated.

"May I have the pleasure, Madam," he whispered in her ear.

"Always the clown," she said. How would she ever know what he was up to. The feelings of paranoia had set upon her again.

Ken had showered and had slipped into some starched and pressed fashion brand jeans, a black tee-top, and a gray sports jacket. His waved back dark brown hair and his clean shaved face gave the appearance of youth and innocence. From experience, Jessica knew that behind those sapphire blue eyes was a devious mind.

When they had eaten and put the dirty dishes into the dish-washer, Ken dropped her off at the lawyer's office. She would worry about getting home later. Mr. Ash met Jessica in front of the building, with his briefcase in his hand. He took her to a local restaurant and they talked while he ate. When he had finished, he got right down to business.

Mr. Ash handed Jessica her mother's will, and turned to a page on which he had highlighted in specific places. "You do realize Jessica your mother was wealthy? Adam is substantially wealthy on his own merit. He will also inherit several million from Jo Anna's estate. You, however, are her prime beneficiary."

"What would happen if my father went to prison?" Jessica asked.

"Everything would be yours in that instance, unless—," he paused.

"Unless what?" she plied him.

"If you were to die, Jessica, as it stands now, everything would go to Jo Anna's and Adam's next of kin. Such kin would have to have proof of kinship.

"Jo Anna was adopted, Mr. Ash. Do you know who her real parents were?" she asked.

"No, but we are looking into that, so far we have come up with a blank. It seems as though Rose and John Hatley made their own adoption arrangements. There may be a record somewhere. I've questioned Adam, but he said, Rose took care of it all."

Meo Rose

"Someone broke into the Hatley House yesterday. Who ever it was, vandalized Jo Anna's room. Do you suppose that that was what they were after?"

"When was that?" Mr. Ash looked up at Jessica with surprise.

"About five pm. I didn't notice it though until about eight pm." Jessica went on to tell Mr. Ash about her unwelcome visitor.

"I've had a guard posted in front of your house," Mr. Ash continued, "so someone must have got in through the back gate, by Joe Santana's cottage."

"I wonder how Al Torres knew about the burglar. I passed out when I found my mother's room ransacked. Someone pulled her picture off the wall and cut it or stabbed it. Al was at Hatley House last night when I woke up" she said. Jessica had hoped he was there for a personal reason.

"Al Torres?" Mr. Ash seemed puzzled.

"Yes you met him at your office the other day. He's a guest at Joe's Cottage." At least that's what she'd been told.

"I'll check that out too. We had better keep our appointment." he paid the bill and they headed to the prison to visit her father.

Sanitary, but very impersonal, would be a reporters description of her father's temporary home. A guard opened a door and let her into a very small room. Two chairs with a table between them were the furnishings. He pointed to a button and an intercom on the wall. "Call me if you need me," he said and shut the door.

Jessica looked at her father. She tried to remember the last time she had seen him, she knew it must have been a much happier occasion. He had aged, and she thought he looked bent and beaten.

"Dear sweet Jessica," he said, "what tangled webs our lives do weave." He bit his lip and tears rolled down his cheeks.

"Daddy." she cried. He managed to stand up, and Jessica went into his arms.

"Oh our beautiful Jo Anna," he cried. He was broken in spirit, and she realized she had never seen her father cry before.

"I will never fill her shoes, but I will try to be a better daughter. Daddy, you'll come home soon." She held him tighter.

"Oh," he moaned. "I have no desire to live without her."

"What about me, Daddy, I miss her too, and I need you now, more than ever." Jessica leaned on her fathers chest and sobbed.

Adam felt his daughter's pain, and he tried to get control of his own.

"Will you stay, Jessica? Will you help me?" He shook her shoulders. Jessica helped him sit down and went around the table and sat opposite him.

"Yes," she said, "but you must help me Daddy. I need to ask you some questions. I need to know, why you were holding the gun?"

Meo Rose

Adam wiped his eyes with his handkerchief. "Jo Anna had given the gun to Joe, about two weeks ago, so how it got there I don't know. I heard the shots and I knew Jo Anna had went out to check on Joe. So I hurried down there, and I found them."

"Why did she give it to Joe?" she asked.

"Some one had broken into Joe's house and the shed, and Jo Anna was worried about him. She was devoted to him you know." Adam rambled.

"Okay, you went down and you found them. So why did you have the gun in your hands?" Jessica was determined to solve the mystery, and some thing just didn't add up, but she just couldn't put her finger on it.

"Someone was there, he dropped the gun and ran. I picked up the gun and I yelled stop. He turned around but,—I couldn't shot." Then Adam collapsed.

Jessica ran to the door and pushed the red button. The guard opened the door. "Get a doctor." Jessica yelled. They put Adam on a stretcher and gave him a sedative to calm him. Then they took him back to his room.

Jessica sat in the hall waiting, finally the doctor came out. "You can see him before you leave Miss, Moore. He's asking for you. He'll soon be asleep."

Jessica leaned over the cot so Adam could hear her. "Daddy, Jessica had to ask him one more question, and he had to tell her the answer, or she wouldn't be able to help him. His eyes opened.

"Where are Jo Anna's adoption papers? Who are her real parents?" Jessica needed this information. His eyes closed again. She pulled her hand away. He opened his eyes and searched Jessica's.

"It's all in the book, in Granny Rose's Journal," he whispered.

Jessica put her face close to his and asked," the autobiography?" He shook his head. "Where?" she squeezed his hand.

"In the shed," he whispered.

She had to ask one more question. "Where are James and Mary?" She squeezed his hand, but this time she got no response. Jessica kissed him and told him she would be back, but she knew he didn't hear. He would rest now, for a while. "Oh Daddy, what is it, why, oh why won't you tell me? She laid her head on his chest and cried. When the nurse came in she wiped her face, checked her lipstick, and walked down the long hall to the outside door.

Mr. Ash was waiting in front of the jail for Jessica. As they pulled onto the turnpike a black suburban followed them until they turned into Hatley Place.

"I'm having Al Torres investigated, if he's involved somehow, it would be better not to tip your hand. Play along until we know more about him. Keep your phone with you, and I'll call you if I learn anything." Mr. Ash did not bother to open her door, but he did watch until she closed the door to the house behind her.

John Ash sighed as he pulled away from the Hatley House.

"Dang," he swore. "She asks to many questions. 'Did he know who Jo Anna's birth parents were?' He laughed. "You'll have to figure it out for yourself Jessica, just as I did years ago." he spoke to the image of Jo Anna he had taped up on the rear of his visor. He laughed again and then he shoved the visor back up. John Ash had an appointment to keep. He turned his car into the North Cathedral Cemetery. "Your father was a sleaze-ball, Jo Anna. He deserved to die. Oh, he had money, and a great position, but he was a sleaze-ball. He paid though, he did, Jo Anna." John laughed as he thought of how he had paid. He noticed the black suburban approaching. He rolled his window down and spoke briefly to the driver of the suburban.

The suburban moved on and John started the engine of his car but before he moved on he pulled down his visor and once again spoke to Jo Anna's likeness.

"Jo Anna, oh Jo Anna, you were supposed to be mine." If only he hadn't introduced her to his friend Adam.

It was early for the happy hour, but he needed a shot or two. He pulled into the Pine-tree Lounge, where he ordered a double shot of Royal Crown.

"Good evening sir," Miranda poured his double shot.

"Have you ever been to France, Miranda?" He asked her.

"No Sir, but it's one of my dreams. Do you know anyone from there?"

"I know a few people." He said. "I have a very rich associate there. J. B. Ansley. Someday I'll make Paris my home. Another double please," he said.

"Tell me about France?" Miranda said.

The lounge was not busy so she listened to Mr. Ash as he talked about his future retirement home in France.

Chapter Eight

Jessica changed into her swimsuit, and stood on her balcony. She couldn't get her father off her mind. It was a man, that Adam had seen in the garden that night. Joe Santana had the gun. Where had Al Torres or whoever he was, been that night? she wondered.

Jessica searched her mind, she grasped for any clue she could find. Her mind returned to her Grandma Rose and Joe Santana in the gardens. She had watched the goings on in the garden as a little girl, and as a teenager. Rose and Joe were friends, no doubt about it. She had watched as they talked and laughed together many times. It seemed as though they had a common goal. Rose kept a journal, and Jessica had seen them share it with one another many times. Jo Anna also shared her grandmother's fondness for Joe Santana, as did her father. Jessica had come upon them all one day when she was about ten.

They had been looking at pictures and sharing something in the Journal.

"Jessica this book is about you," her grandmother had said. "Really Grandma, will you read it to me?"

"It's not finished yet sweetheart, but some day when you are grown and I am no longer here, your mother will give it to you." she had said.

"What is the name of the book?" she had asked her grandmother.

"We are not sure yet," she had said, looking at Joe and Jo Anna for their approval. "We like Jessica's Secret Journal. When you've grown up we'll share that secret with you."

She was grown up now and maybe it was time to find the journal, and learn what that secret was. Jessica was even more convinced that events that took place long ago were somehow connected to what was happening now. It would seem that someone else had an interest in the Journal as well. It had disappeared from the shed.

A movement below caught her eye. Al was opening the gate to the pool. She was drawn to this man in a very unusual way. The recent events though, left very little room for trust. "Play along for now," is what Mr. Ash had said.

She wound her hair in a coil on top of her head, picked up a towel and headed for the pool. She stopped by the library on her way out and listened to a message from Ken. "Gone on a special assignment. I'll be back for the funeral. Save me a seat. Scott is nearby if you need him. See ya."

Special assignment, she thought about the girl in the airport, and laughed.

Jessica went to the bar adjacent to the pool and made a shaker of strawberry margaritas. Al Torres was lounging at the other end of the pool.

"Well here goes," she said to herself. Turning around with a flare she said, "margaritas anyone?"

"Sounds good to me." Al called back. He shuffled over to the bar and carried the drinks to the table. Then at the same time they both turned and dove into the pool. Side by side they swam. As they came out of the water, at the far end, Al eased his arm around Jessica and pulled her to him. He found her lips, and they both sank into the water.

Gasping for air Jessica escaped his arms and quickly swam to the other end, climbed out and grabbed her towel, as she did she knocked his billfold off the table. She reached down to pick it up just as the phone rang.

"Yes, this is Jessica." she sounded winded.

"Are you okay?" Mr. Ash asked. When she said nothing, he continued. "Jessica you may be right about Mr. Torres. We have checked the flights coming from Mexico. We could not confirm any Torres, but we do know an Albert Santana and an Ashley Santana came in on the June twelfth. That was three days before the incidence."

"Thank you, I am with him now." she spoke quietly.

"Please be careful, Jessica." Mr. Ash sounded concerned.

Jessica looked back toward the pool. Al was lounging on a float. She hated to do this but she had to know, so she picked up his billfold and opened it, and there it was. The drivers license was issued to Albert Santana, there was no mistaking that picture. Disbelief came over her. Why, she wondered? What need would he have to use an alias? How was he involved in all of this? She had to find out. She wanted to believe in him. But before she could she had to find out how he was involved.

"Al had climbed out of the pool. Jessica picked up the drinks just as Al approached her.

"Can we walk in the gardens Jessica? There's something I'd like to talk to you about." he sounded serious.

"Can I change and meet you here in thirty minutes?" Jessica asked. She needed time to plan her tactics.

"It's a date," he said. "I'll change and come back for you."

"No——Is that the answer? I don't like that answer. No-one says no to me." He pounded his fist on the bar. You have billions. I thought Jessica's life was worth at least a few thousand."

Miranda watched him as he pounded his fist. Oh no she thought he is out of his pills again. "Hi, how are you tonight. I'm sorry, but I'm kinda busy. A double tonight, sir," she said. She leaned forward so no-one could hear her. "My friend can get you another script for the right price," she told him.

"Not yet." he said. "He's going to pay. Yes you'll see he will pay" And then I won't be hanging around here. France is where I'll go Miranda. Did you know that is where I spent most of my life." He grabbed hold of her wrist, "Will you marry me Miranda? I'll take you to France."

"Where would we get the money?" she asked.

"I'm going to inherit it very soon." he told her.

"Let me know when you do, okay. Miranda excused herself and went to wait on other customers. When she looked back he was gone. France, she thought. Every ones going to France.

Chapter Nine

Jessica changed into a vibrant pink jumpsuit, and let her hair down. She brushed it out and looked in the mirror. Her hair was almost to her waist. Her mother had long thick black hair, and even darker skin than Jessica. Was her mother Hispanic she wondered? Were Jo Anna's birth parents Hispanic? Jessica was sure that the answer would be found in her Grandmother Rose's book.

"Your escort is here Madam." She could learn to like that deep voice.

Jessica pushed the enter button on the intercom. "Be right down sir." She wanted to look her best tonight.

"You are beautiful, Jessica." Al observed.

Jessica thanked him. "What are you reading?" Al had collected the Boston Globe and had turned to the obituaries. She eased up next to him.

Meo Rose

'Mr. Joe Santana left behind two children. A son Albert Santana and a daughter Ashlyn Santana, both of Vancouver, Mexico. He also has six grandchildren.———. He also left many nephews and nieces, who will miss him very much.—Memorial will be on Thursday at two p.m. at St. Mary's Cathedral. He will be buried next to his pre-deceased daughter Anna Santana, at the adjacent cemetery. A meal will be served after the ceremony by the Botanical Women's Auxiliary.'

Before Jessica could speak, Al put his hands on her shoulders and turned her toward him. "There is something I have to tell you Jessica, my name is not Torres, it's Santana."

"But why Al?" Jessica sighed, she was relieved but puzzled. Al didn't answer so Jessica asked him. "Al do you believe my father killed Jo Anna and Joe?"

"No, I don't believe he did, but I don't know who did it or why. I have ideas Jessica, but they are speculations. They won't release Adam on speculations unfortunately." Al thought it might have nothing to do with Jo Anna.

"It's possible that they were after Joe, and Jo Anna just happened to be in the way. I've been doing some detective work, trying to figure out how to get Adam out of jail. Jessica, I know that Joe was afraid of someone for a while before the shooting." Al told her.

"How do you know that?" she asked.

"I have a detective agency in Mexico. Joe invited me over here to stay because he had been being stalked by someone. Some one had broken into his house and work shed."

"Did they call the police? she asked.

"No, but he had told Jo Anna and Adam. They were concerned for him, and they thought they might know who it was. He saw the intruder leaving, and thought he recognized him. That's why Jo Anna had brought the gun to Joe."

"I think my father might know." Jessica told him.

"Why do you say that?" Al asked.

"He didn't kill them Al. He said he heard the shot and came to look for Jo Anna. She had went to check on Joe. When he got to the gardens there was a man there. He threw down the gun and ran. Adam picked up the gun and yelled, stop, whoever it was stopped and looked around, but Adam couldn't shot. So he got away."

"Adam didn't say if he knew him?" Al asked.

"No, that's all he said, and than he just collapsed. They sedated him and he was sleeping when I left. I think he is protecting someone." Jessica was so glad to have someone to share this with. She hoped she was trusting the right person.

"Frustrating isn't it. Lets walk in the garden, Jessica maybe something will come to us." Al led Jessica through the pool area and into the gardens.

It was dark now but the pathways twinkled with tiny lights. The gardens were a tribute to the skilled botanist Joe

Santana and Rose Hatley. Grandma Rose was the inspiration and Joe fulfilled her dreams. They had build a beautiful haven.

The stone walk led to a pond. A wide spread of green curved around the base of the rocks. A white stone settee shaped like a swans head on each end, beckoned them. An arch covered with the brilliant Don Juan rose satisfied the eyes as well as the nostrils of any who would visit there. The garden breathed romance, and dared you to linger, for fear you would fall in love. They dared, they sat down between the curved swan heads. Al held Jessica as gently as she had ever been held, and kissed her as fervently as she had ever been kissed. A tear rolled down her cheek.

"I hope that is a tear of joy," Al whispered.

"It's a tear I had no control over," she sighed.

The moon shed it's light on the clouds and the glittering constellations gave their own radiance to the night. Gazing up at the luminous stars Jessica spotted the Big Dipper. "Oh look," she pointed through the trees. "My father used sit out here with me and Jo Anna. He knew where to find Polaris, the North star, and Orin. Oh, Al, I am going to miss her so much."

He held her tight. "I know you will. We will miss Joe too," Jessica heard his voice crack.

Jessica succumbed to his tenderness, and he let her cry. She reached up to touch his face and tears rolled down his cheeks. She held his face and kissed him until their tears mingled together and joined as one. They lost track of time and finally Al took her hand and led her on through the gardens. "Come," Al, said, holding her arm.

These gardens were special to both of them, because of the lives that had mingled in a lifetime before theirs. Al stopped by one of the ponds. He reached down and picked up two stones. He dropped one in the water. "Now yours," he told her. She took the stone and dropped it. The ripples met each other and twined together and intercepted until they reached the other side of the pond.

"Just like our lives," Al explained. "The ripples made in life may reach areas never intended by the hand that dropped the stone. "Is that it Al? Are the ripples from a stone dropped long ago by some unknowing hand effecting our lives now?" Jessica asked. Al just shook his head as they walked under an arch of ivy and roses. Al picked a rose and handed it to Jessica. His gaze probed her eyes, and this time she didn't turn away.

"Do you know what's happening?" he asked.

"Ah huh," she sighed. She felt like an angel trumpet unfolding its blossoms at night. This was the moment she knew she had fallen in love.

They walked on toward the cottage, where Mr. Santana's family were staying, as guests. As they got near, Jessica stopped in her tracks.

Who Is that?" she asked. There was a man seated on the porch swing. He looked just like Joe Santana.

"Come on, I'll introduce you," Al chuckled.

Meo Rose

The man stood up and reached out for Jessica's hand. "Hello, I'm Albert Santana, and you must be Jessica." He smiled and I knew it was Joe's son.

"Yes, I'm Jo Anna and Adams daughter." She felt the warmth of his hands on hers. She liked this man.

"I can sure see the resemblance of Jo Anna," he told her. "Did you know my mother then Mr. Santana?" If this was Joe's son. Who was Al? Will there be no end to puzzles she thought?

"Actually, I never had the honor, though my Dad adored her and the cottage is filled with her pictures. Would you like to come in, you can see for yourself?"

Jessica had been in the cottage before, with her mother and her grandmother. They had sent her here to bring Mr. Santana food or medicine, when he was ill. He had shared with her how he planted new seed to start flowers for the garden. She had followed him around and watched him work in his shed.

Al lead her to a side table filled with photos in different shaped frames. There were a lot of Jo Anna and Adam, and Jo Anna when she was small, or were they of Jessica. Mostly they were of Jo Anna growing up, and at parties.

"Here's one of Joe and Albert together before Joe left Mexico." Al handed it to her.

"A handsome dude, just like you," Jessica pinched his arm. "Albert is my uncle," he explained. Albert's wife Maria, was my mothers sister. Both of my parents were killed when I was eight. Maria and Albert raised me. Jessica was afraid to look at Al, the tears that she had subsided were surfacing once again.

"I don't remember this picture of me, where was it taken?" Jessica picked up a resemblance of herself when she was about twelve years old.

There was barbs in the voice that spoke from the doorway to the next room.

"That's because its not you, it's me." Jessica turned around to view the young girl who had just spoken.

Al moved across the room and ushered the young girl closer. "Jessica I would like you to meet my daughter Tiffany. Tiffany this is Miss Moore."

"Hello, Miss Moore. Why do we look so much alike? Are you a relative of Mr. Santana's?"

Jessica was speechless. She would like to ask Jo Anna the same question, if she were here. "My mother was adopted, Tiffany, and I don't know who her parents were. Not that I would mind that one bit. We all loved Joe Santana very much."

Al was aware of the forthrightness with which his daughter had handled this new awareness. So he said goodnight to his family and took Jessica's arm and they walked back to Hatley House. "Be back soon Princess," Al kissed his daughter on the top of head before he escorted Jessica back to Hatley House.

As they passed the pond a frog leaped into the water. They paused to look. Jessica had a feeling that someone was making bigger ripples then theirs tonight. She wished she could recapture the romance the garden had held out to them earlier. Reality, however was a little more grim.

Al let her in the back door with her keys. "I want you to know that Tiffany's mother died at childbirth. She has never had a beautiful mother or a grandmother to love her. I'm afraid I've spoiled her. Please forgive her for her rudeness tonight."

"She's forgiven, this must be as confusing to her as it is to me. Thank you for the beautiful evening. I will never walk through the garden again as the same person I was before." Jessica touched his arm with her hand. Al covered it firmly with his other hand. She was aware of the fast movement of her heart.

"Jessica," Al paused, "what matters are the choices we make now. If we let chances slip by without even trying, then what do we have. I don't want you to think I was just lost in the flickering flames in the garden. Jessica, I've fallen in love with you."

"Al, please be patient with me. I've had one whirlwind marriage that failed. I do need your help Al. Help me get my father out of that place, and I'll help you with your daughter. Can we start there and see what happens?"

"That's the best offer I've had today." Al picked her up off her feet and kissed her. Goodnight fair lady," he said, as she shut him out and locked the door.

Jessica sank heavily in her bed. She was seeing ripples, and hers just made a big splash as it hit Al's. She was smiling when she fell asleep.

Chapter Ten

The door chimes woke Jessica. She got out of bed and hit the intercom.

Hello, Jessica, sorry to awaken you. We thought we would get the Mavis's. Will you let us in?"

"Mary is that you?" Jessica yawned.

"Yup, sorry no key." Mary said.

Jessica hit the enter button, and went to take a shower. Her intentions were to be at the Cathredral at ten a.m. She had slipped into a robe and laid out a dress, when Mary knocked on the door. Mary had been her nanny for years and would be the closest thing to a mother she had now.

"I'm so sorry, what a sad situation," Mary enfolded Jessica in her big black arms. Jessica felt like a little girl again, and she let Mary soothe her. Mary trusted James and Mary implicitly. They had worked for her parents nearly as long as Joe Santana.

"Mary, will you help me dress?" Jessica asked.

The phone rang and Mary picked it up and took the message. It was Mr. Ash calling to check on Jessica. Arrangements had been made to get Adam out of jail for the ceremony. He would pick up Adam and they would meet her there. He would need Adam's clothes, and Mary had told him James would drop them at his office. Mary excused herself and soon was back with Jessica's breakfast.

"Let's sit Mary." Jessica said, and walked out onto the balcony. "That's where it happened." Jessica pointed to the spot where Joe and Jo Anna had died. The garden held no peace today, it was as if evil had left it's ugly mark. She looked to the warming sun, but she felt no warmth, she was wounded. She longed for her mother's arms, and she wondered how her father would handle today.

Mary told Jessica, "There is something puzzling me, Jessica, where are Donna and Larry Mavis?"

"Who are Donna and Larry?" Jessica didn't know what she was talking about.

"Jo Anna hired the two of them to fill in while we were gone." I showed Donna around, and James filled Larry in on his responsibility's before we left."

"Did Jo Anna hire them through an agency? Maybe we could check tomorrow. Would you do that Mary? There should be a list of agencies in the kitchen desk." Another question for Adam when he's up to it, she thought. She knew he certainly wouldn't be up to it today.

"Sure Missy, and I'll ask James for sure. Larry may have told him something, it's for sure they have folks in California. They went out there for a few days for some family affair."

"No one has been here since I came in from California, and that was the day after—," She still couldn't say it without tears flowing. She was lacerated by pain.

"Do you suppose they couldn't deal with the shooting, and just left?"

"Did they have the keys to the doors?" Jessica thought about the night she had heard someone in the hallway.

"Yes, we just left them our keys." Mary sounded concerned. "Oh no."

"Some one still has the keys. Someone came in and vandalized Jo Anna's room," Jessica told her. "They came in through the back door."

"What were they after?" Mary wondered.

"We are not sure, and we can only speculate. Mary do you remember the autobiography Grandma Rose was writing?"

"Yes, why is that important?" Mary had seen it many times.

"Adam said there was information in that book about Jo Anna's birth parents. It's possible that they might have something to do with the murder. Do you know where it is?" Jessica hoped Mary would know.

"No baby I don't, and I don't think that is possible." Mary knew who Jo Anna's parents were, but she couldn't say. She had been sworn to secrecy. What about Adam? Have you questioned him about this?" Mary realized Adam was shielding someone.

"He's crushed, Mary, he's sick at heart. He said he didn't want to live without Jo Anna. I'm really worried about him." Jessica told her about Adam's collapse.

"Mr. Ash said he would have a doctor with him at the Cathedral." Mary was glad to change the subject. Come on now baby let's get you dressed." Mary put her arm around Jessica and hoped she wouldn't have to break that promise she had made so long ago.

James brought the limo to the front door, he would drop Jessica at the Cathedral, and come back and get Mary later. "Would you have time today James to do something for me?" Jessica asked as they drove out through the gates.

"Of course, Jessica, anything I can do." James assured her.

"I'd like you to search in the shed for the Journal that Rose and Jo Anna had kept for me all these years. Do you remember it James?" she asked.

"Yes," James said. "I know where she kept it. Joe had used a corner in the shed, to build a giant cedar chest. Rose had kept some of Jo Anna's baby clothes, dolls, and later her prom dresses, pictures and school reports. Later on Jo Anna kept yours there too Missy. They were to be passed on to you someday. Joe kept the key to the chest in the shed."

James had a heart nearly as big as he himself was. Jessica thought this had to be the hardest thing she had seen him and Mary go through in all there years of service at the Hatley House. Of course they had watched Rose and John be buried. That was under different circumstances. But to see Jo Anna cut down in her prime, and Joe,—well that's hurtful. James had thinned, and his hair was pure white, next to his light toned brown skin. James had a look of sophistication, especially today in his gray suit and vest, with the baby blue tie and gold tie clasp.

"If Jo Anna could see you now." Jessica teased him. "She loved you and Mary you know, just like family."

They had pulled up under the vestibule of the North Church Cathedral, attendants were there to greet them, Before Jessica stepped out, she leaned forward and kissed James on his wrinkled brown cheek. "Thank you James," she said. "I am so glad to have you and Mary home."

When she stepped out of the limo, Jessica saw Al waiting by the massive doors of the Cathedral. She felt the quickened flutter of her heart. Al held out his hand to her and together they walked through the Main Hall to view Jo Anna.

"I wanted to share this moment with you," he told Jessica. Last night had changed his course in life. Jessica had instilled feelings that he hadn't felt for twelve years. When Ashley was born and he lost her mother, he never intended to allow himself to ever love again. Jessica had broke through that resolve. Al now had a purpose. Jessica and he had formed a sort of contract. He would do his best to keep his end of the deal. Tiffany may be another matter, he thought. She needed a mother, but would she accept one? Al wasn't sure. He hoped Jessica's charisma would win her over.

"She was a beautiful lady." Al told Jessica as he viewed her mother. "But you are her equal."

"She had so much to live for, she was just forty eight." Jessica touched her long black hair, that lay swirled down around her face and neck. She had climbed on her mothers bed many times and watched her sleep. "She looks like she is asleep," Jessica said. "I feel like any minute she will wake up and smile at me."

"I wish I had known her," Al said.

"Oh Al, why did this have to happen?" she whispered. "Ripples from long ago that finally reached the shore," he reminded her. She turned into his arms and he held her tenderly. "Where are your family?" She would like Tiffany to see Jo Anna for some personal reason, she didn't quite understand herself.

"They'll be here later. I'll join them then," he said as he turned to check out the crowd that were already beginning to assemble. "Well I'll be," Al said. He was staring at a beautiful women that stood next to Tiffany. Ken had already spotted her and made his way to her side. She could have been Jessica's sister, but much older. "Excuse me Jessica," Al turned and went to greet his family.

Jo Anna's old friends approached Jessica and everyone extended their condolences. There were so many stories to listen to she was beginning to feel weak.

A very distinguished man approached her. After viewing Jo Anna, he asked Jessica to step outside for a few minutes. Jessica thanked him for that, because she needed some fresh air. When they were outside, he introduced himself as Mr. Benchly.

"Miss Moore, We are going to miss your mother very much." He handed her a card that intimated that he was the President of the Botonical Society of Boston. "Your mother was the Vice President of our group, Jessica and we would like you to take her position. Don't decide now, but will you consider it, and call me in a few days."

"Thank you Mr. Benchly. I appreciate this, I have so many things to deal with before I could even think about something like this. Besides I have a position with the Long Beach Chronicle." Jessica smiled at him and accepted his card.

"Keep my card, the position will be open until I hear from you," Mr. Benchly saw her father as they drove up and excused himself. "Adam, my man, so good to see you," he approached her father and Mr. Ash, who had just stepped out of the car.

"Benchly, what's new?" Adam returned the handshake.

"I've just asked Jessica to take Jo Anna's place at the Botanical Society. What do you think, Adam?" Mr. Benchly treated Adam with the utmost respect.

"There is nothing that would please me more, but of course Jo Anna and I have always encouraged her to be her own person, and pursue her own dreams. Right now though I would like to be alone with Jessica and Jo Anna." Adam tucked Jessica's arm through his and they walked back inside.

Adam broke up when he saw Jo Anna. He reached out and touched her hand and then he laid his head on the casket and wept. "This is so unfair Jo Anna," he sobbed. "He was always so jealous of my love for you, without reason."

She was shocked at his words, and Jessica assumed he was talking about Joe Santana. Was there a rivalry going on then between Joe and her father? She had to get her father seated before he collapsed again.

A special area was set aside for the family. Mr. Ash and the doctor had been watching Adam and took over. They got him to a seat and sedated him. It was useless to question him now.

Ken came over to check on Adam. He sat next to Jessica and held her hand. Just as she started to ask him about the woman she had seen him with. Adam stood up and pointed to a man in a gray suit. "That's him," he said, and then he collapsed back into his chair.

"Scott, grab the man in the gray suit under the left arch," Ken called on his mobile radio, and then he took off through the crowd. When the man in the gray suit turned around, Jessica knew she had seen him before, but where? The ceremony was about to begin, Jessica looked at Jo Anna, and she almost envied Jo Anna's peace. Her mother was loved by so many, but it seemed there was at least one person who did not share those sentiments.

"We are going to take Adam back now," Mr. Ash said, as soon as the services had ended.

"Will you make arrangements for me to see him soon?" she asked as she walked them to the door.

"I'll call you," Mr. Ash said. Jessica was surprised when he put his arms around her, held her for a minute, and then kissed her on the cheek. "I am truly sorry about your mother Jessica, she was a very special lady. You remind me so much of her."

John Ash was a handsome man. Slightly graying hair, dark brown eyes, a slim physic, well fitted to the expensively cut suits he wore. Adam and John had meet in college and had remained friends and associates since. John had stood up with Adam and Jo Anna when they were married. John was still single.

"We couldn't both have your mother, and I was the lucky one." Adam had remarked when she asked why John hadn't married.

Jessica always had wondered if there was some truth there. It was very obvious that John Ash was a disturbed man.

Was he concerned for his position if her father was incarcerated, or was it more than that. Was he truly grieving a lost love?

Jessica rode in the limo with James and Mary to the cemetery. There were few words spoken. She remembered being at the gravesite. Someone said some words about her mother. She felt herself spinning as if she was being lifted and carried along in the eye of a tornado, and it was about to drop her. She felt herself falling, and then she felt the sting of a needle. Someone with very familiar arms picked her up. She heard someone with a deep voice say, "I love you."

After showing Al out, Mary kissed Jessica on the cheek, pulled her blanket up, turned on the room monitor. "Rest is what you need and rest is what you gonna get, Missy," Mary said as she shut Jessica's door.

After leaving the prison he turned his car back toward the North Church Cemetary. He stepped out and walked to Jo Anna's grave. In his hand he carried a red rose. He kneeled down and placed it at the foot of the marker.

Chapter Eleven

Shock and disbelief had overwhelmed her. For days Jessica's mind drifted aimlessly, she was frustrated by her own weakness. Mary had followed the doctor's orders and kept her comfortable and sedated.

Jessica was awakened, often by some tragic dream, and then there were other dreams. She dreamed of Al and her walking in the garden. She wasn't sure which were dreams and which were reality. When she slept the dreams seemed real and she hoped they would come true. When she woke the dreams had to be battered down.

The smell of sweet roses filled her nostrils before she opened her eyes. A smell that ignited a memory so real that she could feel strong gentle arms around her. A hand touched her arm.

"Jessica are you awake? Mary asked.

Meo Rose

"What time is it? Joe's funeral is today," she sat upright in the bed.

Mary told her. "You've been sick, honey. Joe was buried two days ago."

Jessica sat upright on the bed. "Oh no, I wanted to be there for Al's family."

Mary picked up the vase with the yellow rose in it, and put it up to Jessica's face. "That's okay, Missy, everyone understood."

"What happened to me?" Jessica asked.

"I reckon your body just had all it could take, Missy." Mary said. "That man sure nuf was worried about you. I saw his face, yes soiree, he sure nuf was concerned."

"What are you talking about Mary. What man?" Jessica asked.

"Mr. Al Santana, the young one. He carried you to the car, and he carried you up to your room. I had to shoo him out when the doctor came in. He's been calling every day, sometimes two times, to check on you.——Yes soiree, he cares about you now I say." Mary went on. "James sees it too. He just grins."

Jessica sniffed the rose again, then she read the note attached to the vase. "Good morning Princess," it read. "If you feel up to it, could I have the honor of your presence for dinner tonight?—Love Al."

Jessica picked up the phone and rang the number to Joe's cottage.

"Hello." she recognized Tiffany's voice.

"Hello Tiffany how are you? Jessica inquired. "Is Al around there?"

"No I don't believe he is, and anyway what do you want with my Dad?" she quipped.

"Will you tell him I called," Jessica was aware of the barbs in Tiffany's words.

"No I won't, and please don't call him again. Haven't you done enough harm to our family already," and Tiffany hung up. Tiffany's words were as full of claws as a wild kitten. Jessica put the receiver down and looked sadly at Mary.

"Ouch," Jessica winced.

Mary knew that something had transpired, but could not read the meaning of Jessica's facial expression. "You've had several calls." she said.

"It's time for me to quit dreaming Mary. I'm going to dress, and then I'll return those calls. Have you heard what is going on with my father? Who was the man in the gray suit?" Jessica wasn't quite ready to take on a new problem. She had some of her own to solve.

Mary shook her head. "I'll bring your breakfast to the library, Miss Jessica." "Maybe you should call Scott, he may know."

Mary put a pile of mail on her desk. One of the letters caught her eye. A letter from the New York Mental Institute. "It's probably a bill, she had seen them here before. It no doubt had to do with her half brother. I'll take it to Adam," she said as she placed it into her purse. "I intend to visit him later today."

Mr. Ash made arrangements for her visit with Adam, at three p.m. There was no news of the man in the gray suit, he had told her.

"Do be extra careful, Jessica. Whoever it is may reason to think that Adam knows too much. He may think Adam has told you who it was that was there the night Jo Anna and Joe died."

"That's a question I will ask again today," Jessica told him. She hoped Adam would tell her, if he knew. There were so many secrets that seemed to stem from long ago.

Mary brought a breakfast tray for Jessica. "It's good to see you up and around again."

"I've made some decisions." Jessica told Mary I'm staying here with my father. No matter what happens he's going to need me here. I'm going to call The Chronicle today. I'll ask Randal to send the things in my office and cancel the lease on the condo. My secretary can send my personal things from there."

"I know you'll handle it Jessica." Mary said, "You are Jo Anna's daughter."

Later Jessica drove herself to the prison. Once again the uniformed officer led her to the enclosed room. Adam was waiting with open arms for his daughter this time. "Mr. Ash said you weren't well," he told her as he held her. He gently pushed her hair back and studied her face. "You have your mothers resilience."

Jessica's Secret Journal

Adam sat on a chair, and Jessica sat on the table facing him. "I've made a decision, Daddy. I've called Long Beach and quit my job. When this is all over, I may accept the offer of Vice Chairman for the Botanical Society."

Adam smiled. "Jo Anna would be so proud of you, Jessica. Joe would also. He shared his love for nature, plants, and the beauty of the earth, with you from the time you could crawl. The stories I could tell you." Adam smiled, "I remember him bringing a small toad he had caught and showing it to you and Jo Anna. You could sit up but not walk yet. Jo Anna sat you on a blanket while she read. Joe put the toad down in front of you. When it hopped you squealed with delight, and crawled after it," Adam laughed. "You'll probably find a picture in the Journal. I think I was the camera man that day."

Jessica laughed at herself with Adam. They talked small talk before Jessica questioned him. "Daddy, I have to ask you about Granny Rose's Journal? We can't find it."

"The chest in the shed is where your mother kept it." Adam told her.

"James said the chest was left unlocked and the the key was left in it's door. The Journal was not there. Can you think of anyone who would take it?"

Adam's hand began to shake. He hung his head and stared at his hands. "I need to rest now, Jessica." Adam completely avoided her question. He got up, pushed the buzzer, and waited until the guard came for him.

Jessica reached into her purse for her key. She'd realized she had forgotten to give her father the letter from the New York Mental Facility. She hurried back down the hall and showed the letter to him.

He looked at it briefly and waved his hand in the air. "Will you pay it please Honey?" he said. She wasn't sure he even recognized it. She put it back in her purse, and walked out to her car.

It was a beautiful day to ride, and there was one particular place Jessica was drawn to. The Old North Church was established in 1723. It was one of the oldest historic sites of Boston.

As Jessica passed by the Faneuil Hall, memories of the trips she had taken here with her family to this site, made her sad, until she thought of what her mother had often told her.

"Remember these fun times, sweetheart. So many little girls don't have a family, and so many family's don't have a little girl," she knew now that Jo Anna had referred to her own adoption by the Hatleys.

"I'm remembering Mom." Jessica thought now about another little girl. She thought about the claws in her words and the insecurity in Tiffany's tone toward her. However, she had made a deal with Al, and she had to try, although she didn't quite know where to start. If only her mother were here to help her. She was quite sure Jo Anna would know how to handle it.

She circled Fanuiel Hall once more. She remembered the quaint little shops filled with food, candy, pizza, candy apple, toffee. Her mother had had a caricature done of her once here. She still laughed whenever she remembered that day. She had been about seven years old and had just had a front tooth pulled. She refused to smile, but the artist captured her with the tooth missing.

She had cried all the way home, but her father didn't laugh at her. He just hugged her and said "She's the most beautiful girl in the world, and her mother is a close runner up." Even then Adam had tried to protect her.

"Was that what he was doing now?" she wondered.

Jessica moved on toward The Old North Cemetery. The large metal gate was open. A sign said 'Closes At Eight'. Her watch read seven thirty, so she pulled the car to a stop and walked through the gate. She found The Hatley grave markers. She knelt by her mothers new gravesite. Someone had placed a red rose by her mother's stone marker. She wondered who? Just then a flicker of sunlight on glass caught her attention to a black suburban parked by the fence opposite the gate. It looked very much like the suburban that had followed them before. Fear gripped her, as she walked quickly back to her car, got in and locked the door. She started her car and moved forward slowly. He followed her slowly. Jessica remembered Scott, and she reached for his card in her billfold. She rang the number. After about three rings he answered.

"Scott here."

Jessica let out a deep breath, "Scott, where are you?" she sighed.

"More like, where are you, Jessica? I followed you around Faneuil Hall twice, and then I lost you," he sounded relieved.

"I'm at the North Church Cemetery, someone has been watching me, and he is following me."

"Head toward Hatley house, and turn in as if you weren't aware of him. I'll be on his tail." I'll pick you up on the corner of Fifteenth and Vine street. If it makes you feel better stay on the line," Scott reassured her.

When Jessica pulled in the Hatley gate she saw the suburban move on by, and then shortly a black car moved on by. "I'm gone, Jessica, have a good evening." Scott said, and then hung up the phone. Jessica opened the door and went inside.——

Adam was waiting for John to visit. They had some business to handle. What would he do without John? He had been a real friend.

It was so good to be with Jessica, Adam thought. This has been tough for her. Just a little longer and they would find the son of a gun. Adam slammed his fist on the table in his cell. "I couldn't take a chance on losing her." he cried. Adam thought about that night. He thought about what had been said.

'I didn't mean to do it. I don't know what happened. If you say I did it, I will find Jessica,' he had said. 'I'll find her and I will hurt her. It'll be your fault.'

"What is it you want?" Adam had asked him. It took a while to recognize him with his disguise. But his voice. Adam knew his voice.

'A life, a real life. That's what money can buy.' he had said. 'Maybe France?' he had said.

Adam lowered his head and tears flowed from his eyes.

"How dare you, look what you've done, why couldn't you just take my life not Jo Anna's, not Joes." Adam laid his head on the table.

"John Ash to see you sir." The guard opened the door and let John in. John laid the blackmail letter on the table. Adam looked at it and then he swore.

"That blackmailer," he said. "He won't be happy until he has Hatley Place. A million dollars?——Give it to him, the son of a gun, and then tell him to leave us alone."

"I'll need your signature, Adam, to release that kind of money." John Ash opened his briefcase and laid out a form for Adam to sign.

"First his mother and now him, how did I deserve them?" Adam laid his head back on the table.

"I'll take care of it Adam," John touched Adam's shoulder as he walked away. He told the guard they were done, and went back to his car. Three p.m. He still had time to make it to the

First National Bank with Adams release. He was handed a note for One Million dollars, it was made out to cash. His next stop was the telegram office on the corner of Vine and Cherry. In seconds the note was transferred to the Bank of France, to the account of J. B. Ansley.

Chapter Twelve

Scott Smith had been assigned to the Bovier case by his superior at 'P. I. For Hire'. His previous job with the L. A. Taskforce, made private investigation an oasis of a job. Scott was associated with Ken Moore and Al Santana. Al was usually based in Mexico. Al Santana was in the U.S. by special request and was assigned to his Uncle Joe Santana's case. Ken was assigned to research the birth parents of Jo Anna Bovier. They however would co-ordinate their efforts.

The letter on their desk was from the office of the 'Ash Law Firm'. They were being hired to protect Jessica Moore, who was being threatened, and harassed. Money was no issue. They would be paid a handsome retainer and they would be paid handsomely to fulfill that assignment. Count Adam Bovier would like to talk privately with the assigned investigator.

Scott had been cleared at the holding facility where Adam was being retained. He had been taken to a private room to visit. Respect for one another was immediate. The message that came through to Scott was that Adam loved his wife and daughter very much. If only he had taken my life instead, Adam repeated several times through-out their conversation.

"Jessica must be protected, Mr. Smith." Adam had made that a priority.

Scott sensed that Adam was not completely honest with him. He had a gut feeling that Adam knew who had killed Jo Anna and Joe Santana. That might mean that Adam was being blackmailed. He was willing to pay any amount to protect his daughter. That had come through loud and clear. The possibility was Scott thought, that someone was aware of that and was using it to their own advantage.

'Ken Moore is not to be assigned to Jessica's protection.' Adam had been adamant.

When he had questioned Adam, as to why he didn't trust Ken, he had commented.

'Keep your eye on that one. I happen to know he is money hungry and he is also a playboy.' Adam had just shook his head. 'How my Jessica ever fell in love with him, I'll never understand. That man was checking out our pocket books long before he ever married our girl. But who am I to say, look what I have done.'

When Scott had questioned Ken about the accusation, Ken had a different story to tell.

'It's true,' Ken had told him. Jessica and I did fall in love. 'I blew it,' Ken admitted. 'If the truth was known I still love Jessica. Dang——I love all women.' Ken said, as though it was a deplorable disease.

"The Bank of France, had been receiving large sums of cash deposited into a certain high interest account for over a period of thirty years in the name of J. B. Ansley." Ken continued. "When the deposits stopped the Bank Auditors became suspicious. Our company was called in to investigate. The money trail ended at the office of Adam Bovier. There were no records of such money entering the Bovier bank accounts. It was true that I had made the investigation, but someone in the office of Ash Law Firm had misconstrued the reason for the investigation." For what purpose, Ken had wondered?

Scott had met Jessica, the night her mothers room had been ransacked. Thankfully, he had asked Ken to check on her, when he lost sight of the black suburban that afternoon. Ken was right, he had messed up when he let her slip out of his hands.

"She's a dish. I could go for her myself. Think there's any hope for me?" Scott teased Ken when he called him.

"Don't remind me, I know it well enough." Ken said.

I hate to ask you Ken but all my men are on assignment. Could you make an excuse to keep your eye on Jessica tonight? There is no one else I can trust." Scott asked Ken. Scott intended to stop by a lounge called the Pinetree. There was a couple of waitress's working there that often traded information for money.

Scott pulled into the Pinetree Lounge. He ordered a beer from Miranda.

When he left about a half an hour later he made a call to his supervisor.

"I want a tail on Mr. John Ash. Have him make a full report to me." Scott told his supervisor before he left the office. He would personally check with Albert Santana about the back entrance gate leading to the back door of the Hatley House.

"No stones were to be left unturned," Adam had told him.

Chapter Thirteen

Things inanimate remain to tell the life story of those who pass. Joe Santana was put to rest next to his daughter Anna. Their lives had cast a stone, and made ripples. Ripples that were still felt by those who sat here on this porch, in this swing where Joe had sat just weeks before.

Al, Tiffany and Albert, Joe's son sat on the swing admiring the gardens. "Tell me about Uncle Joe?" Al questioned Albert. He was attempting to fit together the pieces of the puzzle of the duel deaths of Jo Anna Bovier and Joe Santana.

"Joe Santana had three children. Albert, that's me, Ashlyn and Anna. Anna and Ashlyn were twins but not at all alike, in fact they were opposites." Albert told him. "I was eight years older than the girls. Joe and our mother parted ways when the twins were only five years old. To care for his family Joe came to the United States and acquired his citizenship. The

Hatley's gave him a home and a place to work. He remained their faithful employ until his death, in fact, there was a real bond between them that he had never quite understood." Albert paused before he continued. He wondered how much he should tell Al.

"Our mother died when the twins were seventeen. I married, and Ashlyn, a striking beauty was found by a modeling company, and pursued a career. Anna, Ashlyn's twin, was also beautiful in a delicate almost fragile way. She came to the United States to be with their father, Joe Santana. Anna died shortly after she came to the States. No-one ever quite understood why she died. We weren't told why?

"I know about losing someone you love." Al reached over and put his arm around Tiffany.

"I'll never leave you Daddy," Tiffany snuggled over closer to her father.

Maybe he had become overly possessive of her? He thought about how he felt about Jessica. Until now no-one had penetrated the wall he had put up when Jenipher died. He had loved Tiffany's mother, and the loss had left him impotent emotionally. His Aunt Ashlyn had helped him as much as possible, but her career had taken her around the world. So it had been {Me and You Babe} as far as Al and Tiffany had been concerned. Had he damaged his daughter, he wondered?

Death seemed to rule over Tiffany's life more than any fourteen year old should have to bare. Her mother died when she was born. As long as she could remember she had felt guilty for her father's loneliness. She would like to have both a mother and a father, like most of the girls and boys in school. Whenever there were parties, her heart ached for her father. She often lied to him, rather than let him know she wanted to go, she would say she would rather stay with him, but deep inside she longed to be with her friends.

"Has anyone heard from the Hatley House?" Al was waiting for a return call from Jessica.

"Not I," Albert said. "Do I detect a special interest there?"

"Could be." Al said. He kept his eye on Tiffany. He was well aware of her feelings in that area.

At the Hatley House Jessica was working on the deal she had made with Al. She had an idea that Tiffany and Al had developed an unhealthy relationship due to Tiffany's mother's death when she was born. If she was going to compete with a fourteen year old, she would need some outside help. She thought of the Hughes family. Ryan Hughes was a flamboyant sixteen year old, and she thought, he would be just what the doctor ordered.

As the Vice Chairman of the Botanical Society she would have some clout. Every year Jo Anna had sponsored the Botanical Teen Dance, and this year would be no exception. The children ten through sixteen would be invited. They would be supervised by some of the parents, and the pool and garden at the Hatley House would be the setting.

Meo Rose

Jessica picked up the phone. "Mr. Benchley, this is Jessica Moore. I am calling to accept your offer for the position of Vise Chairman. Could I get together with you tomorrow?" Jessica knew Jo Anna would approve of what she was about to do. Her plan was evolving.——

Tiffany turned the letter over and looked at it closely. It was addressed to her. It was from the Botanical Society. She opened it and read the invitation. All members from ages ten to sixteen, were invited to the annual Teen Dance. It would be a formal occasion, to be held at the Hatley House, in the gardens. This year it would be held in honor of Mr. Joe Santana, who had created and maintained them. Albert Santana and his family would be Special guests. RSVP.

Tiffany didn't show her father the letter. She put it under her pillow. That night when she went to bed, she took it out and read it again. She longed to go, but she wouldn't. She would have to show it to her father, since it was in honor of Joe. When Tiffany fell asleep she was drifting across a ballroom floor in a beautiful gown, with a handsome young boy dressed in a tuxedo. She couldn't see his face, but knew he was nice. Just like she had seen on the television.

The next morning Tiffany laid the invitation on the fireplace mantle, and went for a walk in the garden. She floated to the music in her mind, and her feet moved across the garden path in a melodic swing. She hopped up on a bench and was rehearsing a bow. Suddenly, the sound of clapping startled her. "Who are you?" she said, embarrassed by her folly.

"I'm Prince Charles, and you must be Lady Dianna." May I have the honor of this dance? He took her hand and would have swung her in a circle had she not resisted him. Aware that he had surprised her, Ryan apologized quickly. "Don't go its okay, I'm Ryan Hughes. My mother is helping Jessica Moore with the garden decorations for the Teen dance, that we will have here next week," his charm and good looks were impressive. "Are you Tiffany Santana?" Ryan sat down on one of the benches. Tiffany just shook her head. Her awareness of his deep sky-blue eyes left her speechless. Most of her friends had dark brown eyes. Ryan had a rough look, and yet a tenderness that would probably make the girls feel at ease with him, she thought. A sort of James Dean look…she couldn't help but stare at him.

"So, will you save me a dance Tiffany?" he asked her.

"Maybe," she had thought of not going to the dance. She may have second thoughts now though. "I really don't know anyone here," she told him.

"Hey, I have an idea," Ryan jumped up and stood in front of her. "We will be decorating the pool and the gardens next Friday. Would you like to help?"

"You would really want me to?" she felt a funny tingle in her heart, she hadn't felt talking to other boys.

"Yes, come over about ten a.m. Friday." "Oh, I see Miss Moore and my mother, I need to go now." Ryan took off toward the Hatley House. Tiffany watched him go, and she smiled as he jumped in the air and clicked his heels together.

She was still smiling when she ran into the cottage and saw her father with the invitation.

"Shall we go?" he asked her.

"I don't have a formal dress." She tried not to sound too anxious.

"I have an idea," he said. "We'll call Jessica and see if she will help us find one. She'll know what's appropriate. Maybe we can bribe her with dinner." Al picked up the phone and called the Hatley House. When Jessica answered he felt relieved.

"Hello," he said, "Tiffany and I would like to take you to dinner."

"Well, could we make it a foursome and two teens?" Jessica explained that the Hughes were there and they were all heading to Fanuial Hall to shop for decorations for the dance next week.

"Give us twenty minutes and we'll walk over through the gardens." Al turned around to tell Tiffany, but he could already hear the shower running.

The Hughes insisted on driving their car. Tiffany and Ryan had climbed into the third seat. Jessica and Al in back and Sheri and Philip Hughes in front.

They headed directly to Fanuial Hall. The shopping courts in themselves were exciting. Fanuial Hall also held exquisite restaurants. All along the Hall there were roofed counters with bright canopies, where food was being served. The hall lead to the outer gardens by way of arched openings. The metal gates that served as doors at night, were pushed open to allow the flow of the crowds that thronged the market. In the gardens there was music. Artisans were performing for the change dropped into canisters set to be obvious. The atmosphere was one of joy.

Jessica squeezed Al's arm. "Look," she nodded toward Ryan and Tiffany. They had paired off from the adults and were sitting at a fountain, their eyes closed and they were about to throw a penny, to make their dreams come true.

"If only it were that easy, I might try it too." Al gave Jessica a wink.

The restaurant that they choose was as delightful as the Hall. Ryan asked if he and Tiffany could sit in a booth by themselves, so they could get acquainted. Al agreed reluctantly. This is harder for him than it is for Tiffany, Jessica thought. They sat at a secluded table for four. The ambience led toward romance, and Phillip put his arm around Sheri. Al looked back at Tiffany and Ryan, they were laughing, and not at all concerned with their parents. Al tucked Jessica's arm through his and they gave their attention to the menu. Afterward they split up and Jessica, and Sheri went off to shop for a dress with Tiffany.

Tiffany would look like a fairy tale princess in her new gown and slippers. Jewelry was next on the list as they headed to another little store that Sheri remembered. They saw the guys down on the lower level and started down the escalator toward them. Jessica stepped off the escalator and walked toward Al. The last thing she remembered was Al shouting, "LOOK OUT, before she saw stars.

Chapter Fourteen

Scott waited for Jessica to leave the prison. He followed her as she headed past Fanuiel Hall. She parked and he moved past her. When he came around the block he knew he had lost her. He circled the block three more times. Isn't that the way he thought, just get a beautiful girl to tail and then lose her. Finally his phone rang. It's her and someone is tailing her she says.

"Get out of there man, that's my job." he laughs to himself as he sights her again at Fifteenth and Vine. Scott tailed the black suburban. He watched Jessica open the gates in front of Hatley house and close them again as he drove on by.

"I'm gone," he told her on the phone. He called in the license plate number on the black suburban for identification, and held for a name.

"It is rented to a Larry Mavis, sir." The gal at the license bureau told him. He continued to tail it until it pulled into the North Cemetery again.

"You messed up a rendezvous Jessica." Scott said to himself.

He kept driving for about a mile and then he turned around. When he drove past this time he saw the suburban stopped next to a gray Lincoln, and then it moved on. Scott parked across the road just long enough to watch the man in the gray Lincoln get out of his car, and walk to Jo Anna's gravesite. The man in the Lincoln was Mr. John Ash, Adam's attorney. He had seen him with Adam at Jo Anna's funeral.

The phone rang. "Scott here."

"Hey Scott, I've got the ballistic report back on the gun that killed Jo Anna Bovier and Joe Santana. When can you come in?" Sergeant Hanson asked.

"Ten minutes," Scott said and hung up.

Scott wondered about Adam's lawyer friend. Was there something unusual about him visiting Jo Anna's grave. What sort of feelings would cause a man to do that. "Weird," Scott said and made a note of it. Had he been in love with Adam's wife. Scott was having some funny vibes about John Ash.

When he walked into the police station, Sargeant J. D. Hanson pushed a report across his desk. "Adam's gun wasn't the murder weapon. His was a Thirty-Eight Special. The bullets that killed them were from a 357 Magnum.

"Well that's a horse of a different color," Scott replied. The man Adam saw must have had a different gun. But wait Adam said the man he saw had dropped the gun and he had picked it up. He also said that Jo Anna had taken the gun to Joe Santana because she was worried about him. So let's assume that Joe did have Adam's gun. Two bullets were fired, so maybe Joe saw someone and fired. He must have missed, someone may have been hidden in the shadows. Who ever fired at him was more accurate. Jo Anna may have tried to interfere, but of course, if she had seen who it was, she would have taken the second bullet."

"Well one things for sure. There's a 357 Magnum out there with some finger prints on it," Sergeant Hanson said.

Scott called Registrations. When the gal answered he asked. "This is P.I. 53875 Do you have a 357 Magnum registered to a Larry Mavis? While your checking, check on a Mr. John Ash."

"No sir, Mr. Smith. Neither name show a registered ownership. Sorry I couldn't help," the voice on the other end replied.

Sergeant Hanson dashed back into his desk with another report. "The gun was shipped in from France, and was registered to a J. B. Ansley.

"Let's run a check on J. B. Ansley then." Scott said just as his phone rang. "Scott here," he answered.

"Scott, this is Al. We've got trouble here I'm afraid. Jessica's been hurt. We're at The General Hospital near Fanuiel

Hall. She's still in the emergency room. She took a pretty bad blow to her head. She was out of it until a few minutes ago. Dang, Scott I thought she was a goner. You can't imagine the crazy feelings I've been having."

"What do you mean Al? What happened? Scott could tell Al was shook.

"The police are still making a report. They have some eyewitnesses. A man pushed a metal sign over the ledge of the second floor just as Jessica stepped off the escalator onto the first floor. It could have been fatal, man, I feel sick."

"So, then what? Try to settle down, Al. She's okay now, right." Scott was concerned for Al. He'd never seen him so upset.

"Phillip and I were waiting on the first floor. We saw it all happening, but we couldn't stop it. I ran and pushed her out of the way, but she still has a nasty bump on her head."

"I'll be right over, I'm in the car now. Are you in the emergency room?" Scott swung his Mazda 636 onto the highway.

"We are now but they may find a room for her shortly. I'll watch for you. Be careful, man," Al told his friend.

Scott made another call back to the police station, to Sergeant Hanson.

"Hey J. D. this is Scott. "About the attempt on Jessica Moore. Have you got a report yet?

"Yup we sure did. I was going to call you. Where are you?" J. D asked.

"Do they know who did it? Scott hoped.

"There were some eye-witnesses, that are being questioned. As soon as we get the description report, we'll have a profiler do a sketch. It should be ready by tomorrow afternoon. We can publish it. Someone must know this jerk."

"Are you going to release Adam?" Scott asked.

"No, not yet, we think he's safe where he is. If someone else was there, and they think he saw them, then he could pose a threat to them. Well lets say it's one less worry having him where he's at. So until we find the other gun, we'll hold him." Sergeant Hanson assured Scott.

"Gotcha, it wouldn't be a bad idea to put Jessica in there with him," Scott joked.

The Sergeant agreed. "We'll need a statement from Jessica herself when she feels up to it. The Hughes, and their son, as well as Al and his daughter are making statements as we speak." J. D. cleared his voice and then he said. "Al's a hero you know. The way it looks so far is that Al saved her life. If that sign would have fell on her it would have killed her."

"It's attempted murder, I'd say," Scott replied.

"You've got your work cut out for you, Scott. But I hear the pay is good," J. D. chuckled.

"I'd do it for free, I'm becoming attached. I'm at the hospital now and I see Al's waiting for me out front. So long, Sarge." Scott pulled into a parking area and met Al at the hospital door.

Chapter Fifteen

Jessica woke up in an emergency room. A nurse was working on a bag hanging over her head. "This will hurt for just a minute," she said as she stuck her arm with a needle.

"Oh my head," she reached up and felt a cold pack. A brace was around her neck to support it. "What happened?" she asked the nurse.

"You'll be okay now Miss Moore. I'll get the doctor." she pulled back the curtain and disappeared.

Shortly a doctor came in. Jessica was glad to see Al with him. He looked in her eyes with his light. "Good," the doctor took her hand, and at the same time checked his chart. "You've had a bad blow to the head, but on the other hand I understand it could be much worse." he checked her breathing. "I understand this man saved your life, he actually pushed you out of the way. The bump you've got is from when you landed on the floor.

"I just found her and I want to keep her for a while." Al smiled fondly.

"We are going to keep you overnight. We have done x-rays and you have a mild concussion. Does your head hurt?" Jessica just shook her head at the doctor.

"We'll get you something for the pain and the nurse will be waking you up every two hours during the night. So bear with them. We'll probably release you in the morning."

When the doctor had left the room, Al went to the side of the bed and kissed her on the cheek. "I'm leaving now, The Hughes and Tiffany are still in the waiting room. I'll get my car and be back. Don't go away," he stopped at the door and winked at her.

Jessica was put in a private room. A pain drip was inserted into her I.V. tube. She was just dozing off when Al came back. He had Scott with him.

"Do you feel like talking a while?" Scott started. "We seem to be missing something, and we are hoping you can help us. It's up to us to disprove the DA's theory that Adam killed Jo Anna and Joe out of jealousy. So lets see what we've got." He paused and looked at the ceiling.

"One: Someone wanted Joe or Jo Anna dead. He could have killed Adam but he didn't. Adam said it was a man, and we know he recognized him at the funeral. Adam could have shot him in the garden that night and didn't. Sooo!! We think he is shielding or covering for someone. Who? That is the question."

"Or someone may have been after Joe, and Jo Anna caught him and he killed them. I do know Joe was concerned enough to ask me to come to the United States. and spend some time with him. Joe had told Adam and Jo Anna someone had stole something from the shed. He thought he recognized who it was. Jo Anna became concerned for Joe and left the gun with him.

"When did you arrive then Al?" Scott asked. He was taking notes now.

"I and my Aunt Ashlyn flew in together on June fourth. That night Aunt Ashlyn had made a reservation for the Boston Symphony. That was on the fifteenth. Joe wasn't into the Symphony so we went on, after that we had dinner. When we came home it was too late." Al hung his head. "I'll never forgive myself for leaving him that night."

"Did Adam tell you he knew who it was?" Scott asked Jessica.

"No, when ever I got to that question, he fell to pieces. I got the feeling he was protecting someone, but it was just a feeling," Jessica told Scott.

"We did too. Maybe someone he loves is being threatened if he tells. That could be you, Jessica," Scott told them.

"There was one other thing. When Adam saw Jo Anna, he said something I didn't understand. He said, 'this is not fair, he was always jealous of my love for you.' I wasn't sure if he was talking about Joe or someone else." Jessica said.

"One thing for sure, whoever he is, he is mentally deranged." Scott banged his fist lightly on the table.

A light went off in Jessica's memory. "Mentally deranged, oh my land," she tried to sit up. She looked around for her purse. "Did you see my purse?" Jessica asked Al.

Al went to the closet and brought it to her. Jessica opened it and found the letter from the New York Mental Facility. "Read it," she handed it to Al. She watched Al's face and she knew. "It's not a bill is it?" she asked.

"Did you know you had a half brother? Al asked Jessica, as he handed the letter to Scott.

"Yes, why?" she asked.

"They found him missing on the evening of the first day in June. This is a picture of him they published in the New York Times, looking for any clues to where he might be." Scott showed her the picture. "Do you recognize him Jessica?"

"No the man I saw at the funeral wore sunglasses and a French beret."

"Can I take this letter to the police, they could publish his picture in the Boston Globe."

"I think you should show it to Adam first," Al said.

"Okay I'll go see Adam in the morning," Scott got up. "I've got some detective work to do." Scott seemed anxious to get going. "Goodnight Jessica." he said just as his phone rang. "Ken, man, let me call you back. I'll fill you in."

126

Jessica's eyes were penetrating Scott. "Where is Ken?" she demanded.

"He's working on another lead in Mexico. I'll fill you in tomorrow," Scott walked out and she could hear the click, click, click of his shoes in the hall.

Jessica's eyes closed, as the medicine took over, but she was aware of Al's presence sitting next to her bed and she felt secure.——

The scurry of the morning shift woke Jessica. A nurse set a breakfast tray on her table and said, "Good morning Miss Moore," and then stopped by the bed and looked at a chart on the end of it. "The doctor will be in about nine a.m."

Jessica took a brush out of her purse and sat up on the bed. "Ohh!" She moaned as she raised her arm to her hair. So, I guess I'll need help."

Just then Al and Tiffany walked in. "Who needs help?" Al said.

"Can I brush it for you?" Tiffany took the brush, climbed up on the bed and brushed Jessica's long black hair.

"Thank you, Tiffany, I may just keep you with me for a couple of days."

"Would you mind Dad? Tiffany asked her dad? "Anyway Ryan asked me to help decorate the gardens for the dance Saturday evening."

"Oh, how could I manage without you?" Al fained sadness.

Meo Rose

"Could you try just this once." Tiffany teased her dad right back.

"I'll try," he said, and if I can't I'll know right where to find my two favorite girls. Now let me see if I can spring Jessica out of here."

When Al left the room, Tiffany got off the bed and looked squarely at Jessica. "I'm so sorry for the way I treated you on the phone. Can you forgive me?"

"Of course," Jessica reached out her arms.

"Thank you for not telling my dad." she said as she accepted Jessica's hug.

Al walked back into the room. "What, secrets from your Dad."

"We girls have got to stick together." Jessica squeezed Tiffany's arm. When they left the hospital, there was something Jessica wanted to do.

"Could we go visit Joe's gravesite?" she asked.

Al didn't answer, he just turned toward the cemetery. He pulled through the big gate, drove to the new gravesite and parked the car. Jessica took the flowers Al and Ashley had brought her to the hospital.

"Do you mind if I leave them?" She gave them to Tiffany to put on Joe's gravesite. She took one red rose and walked with Ashley to a carved stone nearby. Anna Santana {Born 1935} {Died 1953} "She was just eighteen years old when she died," Jessica said. "That was the year my mother Jo Anna was born."

"Ashley looked at Jessica, "that was the year my Aunt Jo Lynn was born also. She was a twin you know."

"Who told you that?" Was this the day of revelations, she wondered.

"Albert told us," Al said as he took Jessica's hand and walked her back to the car. "You look a little pale, I think we need to get you home."

When they got to Hatley House, Al pulled up to the front door. Tiffany helped Jessica into the library. She propped her up on a daybed, and went to find Mary to tell her they were home.

Jessica closed her eyes. The familio feeling she had for Anna Santana still prevailed. She knew for sure that whatever was happening had begun long ago. Now the pace was quickening as each event moved toward a climax.

Pinetree Lounge had become his second home. He sat on the stool at the bar and downed a double shot of Royal Crown. He got Miranda's attention and asked for another round.

He was deep in thought. Persuasion, Adam that's all it was. Persuasion enough to loosen the grip on your pocket book. "No-one tells me no." He banged his fist on the bar. "No-one!!!!!!!"

Now his demeanor changed. He became sulky and despondent.

"I didn't mean to hurt her, I promise." He talked to his reflection inthe mirror behind the bar, and then he hung his head and cried.

Chapter Sixteen

Tiffany enjoyed playing nurse to Jessica. Mary made lunch for the two of them and let Tiffany serve it in the library. "This is like old times, when Miss Jessica was the nursemaid here. She used to serve her mother and her father in bed, whenever she got in the mood." Mary told her. "Heavens she would have served me, if I would have let her. In fact she even looked a lot like you." Mary went off after that, afraid she had said too much.

The door chimed and Tiffany would have answered, if James hadn't beat her to it. "A box for Miss Jessica Moore." the man said.

"This came for you, Missy." James carried it into the library"

"Just set it by the desk, Thank-you James. "That must be from my office in Long Beach. I'll get Tiffany to sort it out for me."

Tiffany was anxious to help. She got a knife out of the kitchen and opened the big box. "Where do you want me to put these?" she asked Jessica.

"Well the pens and pencils and things like that can go right in the drawer in the big desk. The books can go on that shelf above the desk. The rest just sort on the floor, and we'll put it away later." Jessica told her.

Jessica had Tiffany bring her the briefcase she had left on the side table. She sorted it and laid the Chronical out that had Donna's picture on the front. She had just laid back and closed her eyes, when Tiffany asked another question.

"What is this?" She took the scrape-book to Jessica.

"It's beautiful, I've never seen it before. Where did you find it?" Jessica looked at it closely. It was the size of a large scrape book, but it was covered with a mauve pokadot material. A heart shaped frame was fixed on the top and a picture of Jo Anna or was it Jessica smiled at the beholder. It was filled with many pictures and chapters for different phases of their lives, Jo Anna's and Jessica's.

"It was in the box. It was wrapped in this towel." Ashley handed Jessica a white towel. Long Beach, CA. LaQinta was printed into the corner of the towel.

Jessica looked closely at the cover. Around the heart shaped frame in appliqué was the title. "JESSICA'S SECRET JOURNAL" "Someone left it in my office, obviously, but who?"

Jessica heard the door bell chime. Mary led Al and Scott into the library. She saw the Journal on Jessica's lap. "Oh Missy you found it, Rose and Jo Anna worked endlessly on that Journal." She stopped to look at it closely. "I'll bring our guests some tea, and I'll tell James you found it, he looked for it the other day, you know." Mary very excitedly dashed off to the kitchen.

"Dad," Tiffany ran to greet him with a hug. "Look, Jessica's Secret Journal, somehow it was in Jessica's office in Long Beach.

"What's this all about?" Scott asked Jessica.

"Tiffany just unpacked the things sent from my office at the Chronicle. The Journal that my Grandmother Rose had kept for years was in there. Adam said it was kept in the shed in the big cedar chest. Now how did it get in California? And how did it get in my office?"

Mary came back with a tray of tea and cinnamon toast. She sat the tray on the side desk and poured some tea for Jessica. When she saw the Chronicle, she started to shake. Al took the teacup and handed it to Jessica. Scott cleared a chair and they got her seated.

"That's Donna," Mary pointed to the front of the newspaper.

"Yes, Donna Mavis was her name. How did you know her?" Jessica stared at Mary. Mary couldn't speak. She just shook.

"Go and bring James." Al told Tiffany.

Jessica got up and Al and Scott got Mary to the daybed. James came in and went right to Mary. "What's wrong Mary? What happened?" He looked at Al.

"She saw this picture, and then she went to pieces." Jessica handed the picture to James.

James looked at it. "That is Donna Mavis, the maid that Jo Anna hired. Her and her husband Larry Mavis. Just before we went on vacation."

"But that's impossible," Scott said. "This picture was printed on the sixteenth of June, in California. Donna was dead possibly three or four days before this was printed. But your saying, that she was here at that time."

James sat down and thought hard before he spoke again. "Larry and Donna were here on the second to the fifth of June. Larry called me that night and said his family was having a problem in California. Would I take him to the airport the next morning. I asked if he would be back in time for us to leave on the fourteenth for vacation? He said I could pick him up on the thirteenth. I picked him up on the thirteenth and he dropped us off at the airport on the fourteenth."

"Was Donna with him when he came in?" Scott asked.

"No, he explained she needed to stay another day and he would pick her up when she came in." James replied.

Scott was still writing. "And the next day the fifteenth, Jo Anna and Joe were killed. Did anyone see them here after that?"

"When I came in on the evening of the sixteenth, no-one was here," Jessica explained. "Two days later though someone entered the house and vandalized Jo Anna's room."

"How did you know this woman Donna?" Al asked Jessica.

"Donna came to my office on the eighth of June. She was scared for me, and she warned me someone I knew was out to get me. That must be when she left the Journal on my shelf, above my desk. I got a call from the print room and when I left she must have put it up there before he ushered her out. They were getting on the elevator, and Yes!!! Now I remember the humped shoulders and the beret on his head."

"I think this is the answer. Larry and Donna knew each other at the Mental Institute. Donna was released on the first of June. Larry, or Lawrence Bovier, walked away and talked Donna into helping him." Scott kept writing as he spoke. "He borrowed Donna's last name Mavis, and then finagled his way into the Hatley House. The way I see it timing had a lot to do with it. So when Jo Anna hired them it gave Lawrence carte blanche to the whole place."

"He was mean to Donna. I think she was afraid of him. I heard him pushing her around the night before they flew to California." Mary said as she got up and was busy pouring tea again.

"Lawrence took the journal from the shed, somehow, and finding something with Jessica's address on it, he now knew where he could find her and where she worked. I'd say this Lawrence had a scheming mind. So he went there to get her, but Donna figured him out and took the Journal to Jessica's office and warned her. Something happened to Donna, and your guess is as good as mine. The facts are she was found drown. Now Larry knew he had to be here on the thirteenth. That's why she wasn't with him when he came back. After he took you to the airport, something happened.——Only Adam can finish this story," Scott said.

"The question is how do we prove he killed Donna?" Al asked.

"I know." Tiffany said. Every one in the room looked her as she jumped up and picked up a white towel by its corner, with a Long Beach LaQinta label on it. "Jessica's Secret Journal was wrapped in it, and whoever put it in your office was a guest at the LaQinta motel. I'm betting it was Donna Mavis."

"This is evidence, my dear." Scott slipped it carefully into a plastic bag.

"I'm sure his DNA is all over the Journal as well. I'll have to take it with me to the crime lab? We may have the technician come in and check the room where they stayed. That would put them together here. Now I think we can get Adam released and get some help catching this man before he harms anyone else." Scott was heading out the door before they could say be careful.

Chapter Seventeen

Al walked Scott to his car. They talked about all the new revelations in the Bovier case.

"The black suburban that I've been tailing is rented to Larry Mavis." Scott told Al.

"I think we agree now that's an alias for Lawrence Bovier, escapee from the New York Mental Facility." Al concurred.

"I didn't say anything to Jessica, but I don't think that Lawrence killed Jo Anna and Joe."

"What's your reasoning on that?" Al asked.

"It's just a gut feeling. Also the fact that the murder weapon was a 357 Magnum and that it hasn't been found. It was registered to a J. B. Ansley. Of course Ansley could be an alias for Lawrence Bovier. He lived in France from the time he was five until he was a teenager, with his mother Dorothy," Scott reasoned.

"Well that would change things. If someone else killed them, it's a wonder Lawrence is still alive. That is if he saw someone in the garden that night. Or could it be possible someone was there earlier and Lawrence just happened to came upon him," Al said. "Or maybe it's because someone needs him alive."

"Could it be that he's being used by a middleman to blackmail Adam?" Scott asked.

"Are you referring to John Ash? Do you suppose John's pocketing the money? That would certainly explain why Lawrence would threaten Jessica. It would be a way to get Adam's attention." Al hadn't really like John Ash, or the way he treated Jessica, but all this was just theory and they needed proof.

"I need to see Adam this morning, and dang it, I am going to make him level with me. I've got a little leverage now. We've got the letter from New York, and the picture. If the composite matches, then we've got enough to at least pick up Lawrence Bovier, on attempted murder of Jessica. We could get him in and question him. We may be interested in what he has to say. That way we wouldn't be whistling in the dark." Scott threw a high five at Al before he jumped in his car and took off.

Scott stopped at the Police Station. The composite of the man at Fanuiel Hall was ready. Scott took out the picture of Lawrence to show Sergeant Hanson.

Jessica's Secret Journal

"Bingo!!" J. D. Hanson said. It's a mug match. These profilers do a great job I'd say."

"I'll talk to Adam, today, he's got to level with us. I'll tape a report and we can proceed with our arrest. I'll get back with you as soon as possible." Scott rang the number to the prison to let Adam know he'd be in. Then he stuffed the composite and the picture in a folder with the ballistic report. "This is my leverage, Adam has got to crack today," Scott told J.D.

Adam was waiting in a visitors room when the guard let Scott in. Adam met him with a handshake.

Scott sat down across the table from Adam. Al had called Ash that Jessica was in the hospital, but Scott wasn't sure if he had told Adam. "Has Mr. Ash told you about Jessica?" he asked Adam.

"What about my daughter? She is okay isn't she?" Adam ask. "Ash flew out of the country on some personal business late last night. So now tell me. Where's my daughter?"

Scott wondered if John Ash flew to France? "Adam relax, all is well with Jessica, and she is at Hatley House," Scott reassured him. "She was in the hospital for an evening just for observation, but she's fine. Someone tried to push a metal sign off the second floor of the Fanuiel Hall mall. They aimed to hit her as she stepped off the escalator. Al Santana pushed her out of the way, he actually saved her life."

Adam seemed relieved but now he was angry. "That——. He's been draining me to leave her alone. I've had enough of him. It's time we picked him up."

"You're talking about your son, Lawrence Bovier, aren't you Adam." Scott asked. "Is that who you saw in the garden the night Jo Anna was killed?"

Adam just grunted, "Yes."

"So, you knew he was out of the Institute?" Scott asked.

"Yes, I heard shots and when I got to the garden he was standing over Jo Anna. I slipped into the shadows of the gazebo and watched him. He stooped down and touched her face and then he started sobbing. He was disguised so that I didn't recognize him at first. When he stood up I knew it was him. He has a slight slump of the shoulders, and I knew it was him. I stepped clear of the gazebo and spoke to him. I hoped he wouldn't shoot me too. I said," Lawrence what have you done?"

"I didn't do it. If you tell them I did it I'll—I'll find Jessica and I'll hurt her, I remember he didn't say kill her. His reply surprised me," Adam said. "I asked him what he wanted here."

He said, 'money, a life, France.'

"His words were all mixed up." Adam explained.

"When he dropped the gun I picked it up. I think he thought I would use it to shoot him. He ran through the gardens toward Joe's cottage. I used the phone at the pool bar to call 911. Then I called John, I don't know why, I guess for moral support."

Adam shrugged his shoulders, and rolled his head, as if it felt good to finally tell someone.

"Did John answer, when you called?" Scott asked.

"No," Adam said, "but I left a message and about a half hour later he showed up. He stayed with me while the police did their investigation. We had a couple Royal Crowns before the police arrested me and took me to the police station to question me. It was my gun so they held me until further information could be found. It really did look bad, since it was my gun."

"Did you tell John Ash that you knew it was Lawrence" Scott queried.

"Yes but he promised he wouldn't tell anyone until they picked him up. It was days later that Lawrence called him with a bribe. John brought two blackmail letters on two occasions that my son sent to him."

"How much did you pay him?" Scott was writing notes. He noted the dates and the amounts.

"Ten thousand the first time," Adam sighed deeply, "and then he got greedy and asked for a million, and that was before the attack on Jessica so I figure that John will be hearing from him again, unless we pick him up first."

"Excuse me a minute Adam, I'll get us a cup of coffee and be right back." Scott had been taping the conversation, and now he flipped off the button on his recorder. He walked outside and made a couple of phone calls. One was to J. B. Hanson. "Anything on Ansley?" The answer was no. The next call was to the Pinetree Lounge. After asking for the manager he asked, "Is Miranda in today?"

"Sorry she out of town for a few days. Can I help you?" Mr. Pinetree asked.

"Mr. Pinetree this is Scott Smith, I'm a private investigator, and I hate to tell you but you may have some illegal drug trading going on by some of your employees, and we would like to talk to Miranda when she gets back. Do you know if she is out of the country?" Scott asked. "Oh by the way, what is her last name?"

"Johnson, and as a matter of fact she took off a couple hours last week to get a visa or a passport or some such thing. So there is that possibility. Hey, we aren't going to have any trouble here are we?" Mr. Pinetree said.

That was what Scott was hoping for. "No sir, not if you cooperate with us, and your not involved yourself. What I want is for you to see if you can find out where she is and who she is with. I have a feeling it is with one of your regular customers. As soon as she gets back we would like to pick her up and question her. We want to take her by surprise so she can't tip off anyone she might be involved with. Could you give me your word that you will notify me as soon as she's back, and that you won't tell anyone about this?" Scott gave him his cell phone number and hung up.

Adam was waiting at the door when Scott brought two cups of hot coffee back to the visiting room.

"I've got some news for you Adam. You better sit down," Scott sat down again himself.

"What now? Adam said, as he seated himself across from Scott.

Scott laid out the profile that Hanson's crew had produced from the eye witness report. "This is the man that was seen pushing the sign onto Jessica at the mall." Then he laid out the New York Newspaper with Lawrence's picture on the front. "A pretty good match isn't it?" Scott said.

"Wow," was all Adam could say.

"We'd like your permission to run these pictures in the Boston Globe. Some one will recognize him and maybe we can pick him up peacefully." Scott said as he folded the pictures and put them back in his file.

"As long as Jessica's in a safe environment," Adam said, "That's fine with me. He needs to fess up to what he's done."

"Do you own a 357 Magnum?" When Adam shook his head no, Scott continued. "Adam, the ballistic report shows that your 38 Special did not kill Jo Anna and Joe. They were killed with a 357 Magnum."

"Wow, I've had a while to replay the events of that night. I remember there were two shots, pop, pop, and then I started down the stairs and I heard two more shots." Adam said.

"Adam, I'm taping all of this so we can play it back later, it could even be used as evidence, is that okay?"

"Yes anything to get that——son off the streets." Adam's demeanor was showing stress.

"Another couple of questions and then I'll go. Tell me about John Ash? Do you trust him?" Scott took Adam by surprise. "I've had no reason to not trust him." Adam said.

"How did he feel about Jo Anna? Scott questioned.

"He loved her. He knew her before I did, and I think he never quite got over her. In fact he introduced her to me. It was mutual love for both of us. I guess maybe he felt jilted by her, but she had never gave him any reason to think she cared that deeply about him. When Jo Anna and I married he was my best man."

"Why did he come to work for you and Jo Anna?" Scott wondered why a man would torture himself in that manner?

"He went through a period of depression after college, when his dreams seemed to fall through. He did get involved with a girl out of college. I'm trying to remember her name. It was Jenny—or Jackie—ah, can't think of her last name. I believe I heard that she married and moved off somewhere. Anyway he needed work and we needed a new lawyer after Rose and John Hatley were gone. He takes care of all of our affairs." Adam wondered what John had to do with all of this?

"That's what I've been told. Adam, do you know anyone by the name of, J. B. Ansley?" Once again Adam shook his head negatively.

"The gun that shot Jo Anna and Joe was a 357 Magnum registered in France to a J. B. Ansley. Scott stood up. "So, we've

144

got a tail on this Ansley and we are going to work on picking Lawrence up. Sargent J. D. Hanson hopes you'll be patient a little longer Adam, and we should have this all wrapped up." They walked out together, shook hands and the guard took Adam back to his cell.

Scott went directly to the Police Station. J. D. Hanson greeted him and they sat down to go over the report. The tape and the new report was filed. Request to release Adam as soon as Lawrence was picked up was made to present to the Judge on the next day. Scott then drove to, P. I for Hire, and made a full report to his supervisor. "I want permission to tail Mr. John Ash to France. I'd like to check on his whereabouts, and his finances." he told his supervisor.

"Permission granted," he said, "just be careful and keep your cell with you. I'll have some backups ready by the time you get there. Maybe they can do some leg work and meet you when you land." Benchly stood up and shook Scott's hand.

"Will you have Jean, the office girl, get my tickets and throw some weight around and find out where John Ash and Miranda flew into and make my flight similar? I'll need all the help I can get," Scott told his supervisor.

"You've got it. It's as good as done." Benchly called Jean in and gave her the instructions.

"I'll be back as soon as I fill Al Santana in on the latest, to pick up the tickets." Scott said as he walked out the door. He phoned Al and caught him at the cottage. "We are picking up Lawrence, and Adam should be home later today. But let's surprise Jessica, just in case there's a mess up somehow. See you when I get back.

"Oh by the way, I heard from Ken, he should be flying in from Mexico this afternoon," Al chuckled. "He loved his assignment and he says to tell you that he accomplished his commission."

"Whoopee" See you man, I hope I do as well." Scott hung up.

An hour later Scott cleared his gun at the ticket counter, and got on the next flight to Paris, France. His gun and his papers he needed were in his brief case, which he tucked under his seat. His change of clothes pushed into the overhead bin, he sat down to relax. When the flight attendant came by he showed her some attention, and asked if she could pull up the itinerary for the last flight to Paris.

"Got a gal heading over ahead of me," He gave the attendant a wink. Be right back she said and shortly she handed him a readout of the last flight.

"Bingo" he said as he found the names John Ash and Miranda Johnson. Between snoozes Scott sorted out his priorities. His first step would be to find where Mr. J. B. Ansley did his banking. He slapped his briefcase, in it he had a picture of Mr. John Ash, he had taken from the Boston Globe, which had featured the Jo Anna Bovier's funeral.

Chapter Eighteen

Tiffany had left the nursing to her Dad and fled to the gardens to be with Ryan. They, along with some other teens, could be heard in the background. Hatley house sounded as Jessica remembered it, for the first time since her arrival from Long Beach. Scott had returned the Journal and he was hopeful that the information in the Journal would free Adam. Some of it he said was very compelling. He thought she should read it carefully. After he left Al came back into the library and sat on the couch with Jessica.

"Can I stay with you while you read it? Al asked her. She lay with her back against his chest, with her Journal on her lap. She held the Journal close to her heart with both arms. Her grandmother Rose and her mother Jo Anna had left this token of love, for a day when they could no longer sit beside her themselves.

"I will cherish it forever," a tear crept down her cheek and dropped on Al's arm. He pulled her closer, and buried his chin in her neck.

Jessica felt melancholy, as she leafed through the Journal. She especially felt the familial undercurrent as she opened the Journal to the chapter entitled "Joe Santana" This was Anna's father, and Jessica felt the same connected feelings she had for Anna earlier. She fingered the facial profile on the picture. Joe Santana was handsome, almost debonair. His deep brown eyes, not unlike her own, a dominant trait he had passed on to his children, and his grandchildren. She would have liked to known him as a young man. No doubt that is why her grandmother Rose made the Journal. "I wonder why he never remarried?" she asked Al.

Al traced Jessica's face with his hand and then he cupped it gently and leaned forward to kiss her gently on the cheek.

But you didn't answer my question?" she was not wondering now about Joe, but about Al. "Why didn't you remarry, after Tiffany's mother died?"

"Tiffany's mother was special and when she died it left a hole in my heart, and until now there has been no-one that has come close to filling it." Al turned her so he could look deeply in her eyes. "I love you," he whispered.

Something happened to Jessica in that moment in time, an awareness that was electric. The night in the garden she had felt that way, but there had been the stars, and the flickering candles, and the smell of roses. Now there was none of that. There was just Al and Jessica, and even without the ambiance, she gave herself over to an awareness of a woman, who could after all fall in love. "I love you too," she whispered. Jessica felt the beat of his heart, and hers as they beat in rhythm.

After a while, Al spoke again. "Maybe the Journal will answer your question about Joe. They lived in harder times, you know."

Jessica turned to a Chapter Fourteen entitled, "Joe Santana."

The depression of the Second World War affected everyone. Joe and Lynn Santana already had an eight-year-old son Albert. In 1935 Lynn told Joe she was having twins. Anna and Ashlin were born on Dec 10, 1935. Times were bad. There was no work. Joe had the opportunity of coming to the U.S. He became a citizen and the Hatleys gave him a home and work. He was able to send money to his wife Lynn to care for the children. The twins were seventeen when their mother died. Before Lynn died she wrote this letter to Joe.

Dear Joe, 1952

I am sending Anna to you. She needs you now. Anna is pregnant. She is not a bad girl; a married man raped her. We have not even told him, but you can see she needs to leave here now. No-one is aware except Anna, me and now you. Ashlyn is staying with my sister, she is the strong one. I have no fear for her. Already she has signed a contract with a modeling company. Thank-you for all the care you've shown us. I say goodbye a little easier knowing Anna will be with you. Love Lynn

Dear Lynn 1953

I am so sorry Lynn; even though you are not here I must write this. I have let you down again. In a way I am glad you are not here to bear this burden. Anna was so frail. Both physically and emotionally she could not bear the burden that was handed her. She died when her twins were born. They said it was her heart, and I agree, a broken heart, though, is what I say. She never got over losing you, and she blamed herself for your death. I have named the twins after You and Anna, and Myself. I pray that they will have a much richer life than we. Jo Anna and Jo Lynn are their names. Jessica couldn't see to read any further. She handed the Journal to Al, and he continued.

PS: Rose and John Hatley have helped me through this trauma. They are going to adopt Jo Anna as their own. That means I will be able to share her life even though we won't tell her until she is older that I am her Grandfather. Note: Your sister Grace and her husband has asked to Adopt Jo lynn. They have asked that I have no contact with her and I have agreed.

It is the wish of Rose and John Hatley that this Secret Journal along with it's pictures will be given to Jessica, Adam and Jo Anna's daughter at some point in time by her parents. Jo

Anna's twin sister Jo Lynn is Jessica's Aunt. We have not had any contact with her since they took her home to Mexico.

"I wish I would have known him when he was young. I had a feeling of family when I was at Anna's grave the other day." Jessica cried on Al's chest and he held her tenderly. "So that means I have an Aunt Jo Lynn somewhere. I wonder if she looks like my mother? I would like to find her. Would you help me?"

Before Al could answer someone rang the door chime. James came into the Library with Scott. "I have a surprise for you Jessica."

Jessica looked up to see her father coming through the door. She flew into his arms, and he cried with her. After a few minutes, they relaxed and Mary fixed some snacks and hot tea. "You know Lawrence is being picked up, and he will be tried for Joe's and Jo Anna's death, as well as Donna Mavis's," he told them all. "He threatened to kill you Jessica, too if I went to the police, so I had to wait it out. I was so afraid for your life Jessica, and I'm so glad that it's over."

Ryan and Ashley came into the library to ask if they could go swimming. When Adam saw Ashley, they could hear the soft gasp of breath he drew in. "This is my daughter Ashley, Adam. Tiffany come and say hello to Jessica's father, Adam," Al introduced her.

"I'm sorry if I stare Tiffany Adam apologized. "It's just you look so much like Jessica did at your age."

"There is something I want you to see," Jessica made room for Tiffany on the couch by her. "This is a picture of Mr. Santana when he was young." Jessica handed her the picture of Joe. "Remember when we were at Anna Santana's gravesite? She died in 1953, and I told you that was the year my mother was born. Anna died in childbirth just as your mother did. She was Jo Anna's mother and my grandmother."

"I wish you were my mother," Tiffany reached out her hand to Jessica.

Jessica pulled her into her arms; tears ran down their cheeks. Al went to them and cried with them. "Jessica will you marry us?" Al took her hand and placed Tiffany's on it, and waited for an answer.

"Yes, Yes," she answered. She guessed the reverberations of what had transpired here would echo through time to touch a generation not born yet.

After Ryan and Tiffany went to swim, Jessica told Adam about the Teen Dance to be held the next day. He was pleased to have her continue in her Jo Anna's footsteps. Adam excused himself and went to his room to relax. Jessica called Mary and made arrangement for a family dinner to be served at seven p.m. in the main dinning room.

"I want to go to my room and prepare for tonight," Jessica told Al as he walked her to the elevator. He would collect Tiffany and they would be back at seven.——

Jessica had called Albert Santana and invited him to dinner. "I'll come with Al and Tiffany. Thank-you. I'm looking forward to meeting Adam Bovier."

Ryan and Tiffany had put the finishing touches on the decorations. The gardens were delightful. Floating candles were ready to light and slip into the pool. The fountain was set to changing lights with variations of colors to give a special ambiance. The bushes and shrubs twinkled with tiny lights.

The dining room was buzzing with activity. Green salads and crusty loaves of whole grain bread had been placed on the table. Candles flickered from the gold centerpiece. A central table had been decorated in the grand entrance room, for the event the next evening. James was serving cocktails or punch from two large crystal punch bowls.

Adam dressed for dinner and as he stepped off the elevator, Albert Santana had arrived through the patio doors and was being served a cocktail. He went to greet him immediately. The likeness he saw to Joe Santana was as shocking as the likeness he had seen in Ashley to Jessica. "Good to have you home, sir," James welcomed Adam. "This is Albert Santana, Joes son." he introduced Adam.

Adam took a martini and he and Albert found a settee and made themselves comfortable.

Ryan had been invited to dinner and he and Tiffany had found a chess game in the family room and were enjoying themselves.

Mary rang the bell for dinner, and everyone was drawing close to the dining room. They all turned when the front door chimmed. James opened the door.

"Ken, what ever are you doing here?" Jessica asked, surprised he would just show up now.

Ken stepped in and with him was a very beautiful woman. She looked wholly Spanish. Her hair was coiled on the back of her head, in a way only a beautiful face could be displayed. Her head rose proudly, her chin lifted, luminous eyes raised to search us out. Her dress was brilliant. Flamingo styling with a wide gold belt, and flashy jewelry on her wrists and neck.

Jessica wasn't surprised to see Ken with a woman but his next words left her flabbergasted.

"Adam, Jessica, Al, Tiffany," he looked at all of us, and than he took the woman's hand as he told us her name. "This is Jo Lynn Sanchez. She is Jo Anna's twin sister. She doesn't speak good English."

"Hola," she said.

Jessica went to her side and put her arm around her shoulders. "Welcome, we were just going to eat, Mary will set two more places. Join us Ken and tell us where you found Jo Lynn."——.

Chapter Nineteen

Agent Tim Hodges, based in Paris, waited for the flight due into Paris, France from the United States. His call from the Supervisor Benchley, of 'P. I. For Hire,' gave him heads up on his next assignment with Scott Smith.

The secretary at the office had searched the yellow pages and the major banks and stock agents. Some of them had been through analysis, and were deleted as to possibilities. There were two Ansleys listed that had any potential. The banks were a different story, there were many, that held accounts for J. B. Ansley.

Tim had wrote the two addresses down and brought them with him. Benchley had specified that time was of the essence. He had been told to look for two major deposits to Ansley. He had found two that had matched exactly at the Commodore Bank and Loan. It took some doing to get the bank officer to allow him to make a copy of each one. With some help from his P. I. Card and a call from the chief, he got the job done.

Tim held a sign with Scott Smith written on it. Scott spotted it instantly.

They shook hands and headed to a nearby sidewalk grill for some breakfast. Tim handed the bank reports to Scott. "Bingo," Scott said as he looked at a deposit for ten thousand, and one for One million. Next they headed to the names on Tim's list. They would use John Ash's picture, and blitz the area near the Ansley home.

"We'll try the one on Queen Street. The homes are substantial but not obnoxious." Tim said as they pulled past 1501 Queen Street. Tim pointed it out to Scott as they passed on by for a block, parked and headed toward the first house they saw. They walked up the stairs of a big white house with black shutters. Scott rang the door bell, and talked to an older woman around fifty.

"Sorry to bother you Madam, but we are searching for this man, Scott showed her the caption in the Boston Globe that Scott had carried with him with John Ash's picture.

She looked closely at the picture and said, "no sir, I haven't seen him around here. His face does look familiar. Probably saw it in the society section."

They got a similar reaction at the next home, so they moved on to 1501 Queen Street.

"Hello," the stout woman said as she pulled her robe closely around her. She wore no makeup.

"Madam, are you Mrs. Ansley?" Scott asked.

"Yes sir," she said. "Can I help you?

"Yes, we are looking for a J. B. Ansley." Scott told her.

"My husband was J. B. Ansley, but he's been gone for six years now. Can you tell me what you want with him?" she asked.

"We had a mutual friend and thought we would stop and say hello while we were here. Did your husband travel often?" Scott asked.

"Oh, no sir, you must be looking for the J. B. Ansley in the Creasant Ridge area. Out at Lake Benson. I believe there is a Jacquelyn Ansley, who used to be a movie star of a sort."

"Thank you madam. We'll stop over there and say hi." Tim told her. He knew the area she meant. They walked back to Tim's car and headed toward Lake Benson.

The house was beautiful, and the yard was exclusive. A circle drive lead to the front double door with side lights. They drove up under a vestibule. Sculptured with shrubs and Japanese Maple. Terrazzo decking formed a large covered outer foyer. Hugh pots of azaleas and geraniums gave contrasting coloring. Hanging petunias and ferns decked the walls of the foyer.

Scott noted a ramp that led down one side of the deck to the driveway. He pointed it out to Tim. "Someone here uses a wheelchair."

Scott pushed the doorbell and listened to the mellow chimes, just as the door opened. An attractive, blue eyed, long legged French maid opened the door.

"Sir, may I help you," She said in very good English.

Scott caught himself starring. "Sorry, you took me by surprise, I expected to have to translate some French," Scott gave her a big smile. Hi, I'm Scott Smith and this is my partner Tim Hodges."

"I'm from the United States, I'm an artist and trying to work my way through school here in Paris. Also I travel to the states with the Mistress Ansley often," she said. "I didn't mean to be rude, I'm Connie Harmon, Miss Ansley's maid. Can I tell her why you're here. She's with her son at the moment."

"Just tell her we are investigating some resent thefts and would like a moment of her time." Scott told her as he checked her over, and liked what he saw.

"Would you like to step into the foyer, and I'll see if she will see you." Connie Harmon showed them in and turned around and left the room.

Shortly a tall slender figure of a woman appeared in the doorway. A curious look on her face that turned more to surprise. She noticed we were studying the pictures on the wall.

"Are you J. B. Ansley?" Scott asked.

"I'm Jacquelyn Ansley, what is it you want?"

"We are investigating a crime, Mrs. Ansley. It is Mrs. Ansley isn't it?" He questioned her.

"Sir Jacquelyn B. Ansley has been my name from birth." She was starting to look very nervous.

Scott didn't want to anger her, he had a few more questions. "Do you ever travel to the United States, Jacquelyn?"

"On occasion," she said.

"When was the last occasion?" Scott could tell she was getting antsy.

"I can't really recall the last date, and I think I've said enough. I'd like you to leave." Jacquelyn got up and started to leave. She turned to tell him again to leave, but his next question surprised her.

"If I could just get you to suffer me one more question." Scott looked into her eyes intently. "Do you own a 357 Magnum?" he queried.

"As a matter of fact I did own one but it has been stolen. Why do you ask?" She knew John had taken it to his home in the states. She didn't know what he had done with it after that day.

Scott was about to pull out John Ash's picture when a young man, about thirty he guessed, wheeled his chair up behind Jacquelyn Ansley.

"What's going on mother, is everything okay?" he asked.

The man reminded Scott of someone he knew. He'd remember in a minute he hoped.

"This is my son, Ashley Ansley," she introduced him.

Scott wondered if this could be John Ash's son too. Ashley, after his father? Could be."

"We are investigating a duel murder of a Jo Anna Bovier and a Joe Santana."

"What does that have to do with us?" Ashley asked Scott.

He recognized him when he scowled. John Ash's son, he'd bet on it. "I'm hoping it doesn't. The murder weapon was registered to a J. B. Ansley here in Paris France."

Jacquelyn set muted, and her son stared at her. "Like I said it must have been taken, and I haven't seen it in a while."

"We'll be glad to make that report for you. Well, we'll be going then. Thanks for you cooperation. If you can think of where the gun may have been left or who may have taken it, please let us know. You can just call the police station, they'll know who to locate."

Tim reached out and shook hands with Ashley. Scott reached into his briefcase and pulled out John's picture.

"By the way, do either of you recognize this man? Scott watched their reaction.

"No sir, I can't say that I do" She turned to stare at her son.

"How about you Ashley?" Scott waited. Ashley just shook his head no.

"Okay, well we'll go then." He looked directly at Ashley again. "Can't remember where, but I feel like I know you. Hum, well they say we all have a double somewhere."

"We'll show ourselves out," Tim got up and headed across the foyer toward the front door.

Scott felt in his gut they were lying, but how would they prove it.

When they reached the front door he looked around for Connie. She was waiting for them by a bush that shielded her from view of the foyer window. It was obvious she wanted to tell them something, but she was scared.

Scott handed her a card with his cell number. "Do you know what it means to be an accessory to a crime Connie?"

"I think so sir," she said.

"It means to cover up information that could be used to solve a crime." Scott liked Connie, he would like her much more if she leveled with him. "Do you follow me Connie?" Scott liked her intense blue eyes.

"Yes sir," Connie said. "I get off work at twelve o'clock. Can I call you?"

"We'll be waiting." Scott reached out and took her trembling hand. He could sense her fear, and he wanted to reassure her she could trust him. "Could we take you to lunch?"

Connie shook her head in the positive. "I'll call when I leave," she said.

Scott and Tim drove back toward town and turned into a French Courtyard restaurant. They had just seated when she called. She understood where they were and could be there in fifteen minutes. Tim checked his watch and finally went to the front to meet her.

She slid in the booth between Tim and the wall. She had donned dark glasses and fixed her blond hair into a twist. Disguise—Scott thought. Across the table Scott laid out the news article of John Ash. Then he laid out the profile of John.

"Connie we will be taping our conversation," Scott showed her the recorder in his pocket. Don't be nervous. From here on in you will be protected, as a witness in a murder case would be. We are simply after the truth as we believe you are."

Connie stared at the pictures, but still she paused. Finally, she looked up at Scott. "Sir that is Mr. John Ash, he is Ashley's father."

"You're very certain of that?" Tim asked. He was taking notes while Scott concentrated on the interview.

"Oh yes, he's been here many times since I've been working for Mistress Ansley, within the last three years. You see Ashley wrecked his motor cycle, and spent a year recuperating. Later when he finally came home, there was corrective surgery, one after the other. Jacquelyn couldn't have maintained her life style and paid the bills for Ashley's surgery if Mr. Ash hadn't helped her."

"How do you know that? Tim entreated. "I answered the door when a cable was delivered. When I took it to her she read it quickly and then said. 'Great, now we can afford to have that surgery for Ashley.' She asked me to get her the rolodex off her desk and she made a call to Ashley's doctor."

"When was the last time he flew in?" Scott inquired.

"He was here yesterday, but didn't stay long." "Did you notice anything unusual, anything that might relate to this investigation? Scott touched her hand lightly, this is going well he thought.

"Sir you mentioned the 357 Magnum, when you questioned Jacquelyn. I saw Mr. Ash go to the gun cabinet and take something out. I was just coming in to see if they wanted some tea. His back was to the door as was hers. But I watched him as he used the key to relock it, and then lay the key in front of her at the table.

"When did John leave for the United States?"

"He took the red eye out late last night. I heard him tell Jacquelyn that he would get some sleep on the airplane." Connie excused herself to use the restroom.

Soon she returned and took her spot next to Tim in the booth. Scott had one more question and he motioned for Tim to turn the recorder back on.

"Jacquelyn never married Mr. Ash. I wonder why? Do you have any idea Connie?" Scott invited her response.

"One evening I caught her crying by herself in the living room. Ashley was in the hospital and she seemed so lonely. She invited me to sit with her. She talked about her deep love for John, that's what she called him. I asked if there was any chance that someday he might stay in Paris, and they would marry?" Connie caught her breath. "She said, 'maybe if Jo Anna Bovier was out of the way she would stand a chance.' She seemed real bitter, when she said it."

"Would you repeat what you just said? Scott interrogated.

"You mean about Jo Anna? She said that maybe if Jo Anna were out of the way she would stand a chance." Connie answered.

"Wow Connie, I want you to look at this calendar. Do you recall the last time that Jacquelyn was in the United States with John?" Scott asked.

"It was on the thirteenth of June. She had just came in from visiting Ashley in the hospital. She seemed very depressed, and I remember asking her if Ashley was alright? She asked me to go and visit him for the next few days, and to tell him she had went to get his father, that she would be back in a few days. I took her to the airport and dropped her off. She would have been in the United States on the fourteenth of June."

The waitress came by and took their empty plates, and refilled the coffee cups. After she left Scott continued. "Connie," he said, Jo Anna was a beautiful woman and Joe Santana was devoted to the Bovier family for years. They didn't deserve to have their lives cut short. The 357 Magnum was Jacquelyn Ansley's. Jacquelyn Ansley knows more than she is telling. I am going to have her and her son picked up for questioning. We can hold them until the gun is found." Scott once again gazed intently into her eyes. He wanted to protect her. He had to protect her but how was he going to do that if he left her here in Paris.

"I don't want you to go back there, it could be dangerous. Would you consider going back to the United States with me? You could stay at the Hatley House with Jessica for now," she could use some company Scott thought. Scott took her two hands, that felt very cold, between his and squeezed them.

Connie looked into Scott's probing eye's. She trusted this man and she felt that if he asked her to go to the moon with him she would. "My mom lives in Sunnyvale, California. Can I call her from Boston, she'll understand if she knows why I'm there. She believes in justice, and has always taught me to stand up for truth."

"We'll see to it," Scott assured her.

Tim was on his cell phone making plans for Scott and Connie's flight to the United States. "Flights at five," he told them after he hung up.

Scott's head was spinning. "Can you meet us here at four," he asked Connie. There is something that has escaped me," Scott said. "Miranda Hodges, where is she? She flew in with John Ash. Did he bring a visitor to Jacquelyn's with him?"

Connie looked puzzled. "No," she said.

"Here is the itinerary Tim, you'll have to check on that." Scott handed it to Tim. "Pull some punches and see if she flew back with Ash. She may have known to much. That's why you are going with me." Scott smiled warmly at Connie.

They parted and Connie went to pack up some clothes, and Tim and Scott went to the police station to make their report. By the time they left to pick her up again, three police officers were leaving with a warrant for Jacquelyn Ansleys arrest. They soon arrived at the airport, found their gate and checked their luggage.

Tim flipped fifty cents into a vending machine and took out a paper. Their flight was being announced over the intercom, so Tim handed Scott the newspaper. Scott grabbed his briefcase and he and Connie headed for the aircraft.

Tucked into their first class seats Scott proceeded to tell Connie about their case. He enjoyed her company and soon they were laughing about the coincidences of the day. They giggled like two kids when they talked about the likelihood of the two of them being on this flight together, since they hadn't known each other more than eight hours.

Before they dosed off to sleep, Scott took her hand in his. "I like you Connie. You're a good sport."

I can't believe my luck she thought. "I kind of like you too," she replied.

When the lights lowered they fell asleep.

Chapter Twenty

John Ash was always glad to see his son, Ashley. His sunshine in a dark world. The last thirty years had been spent assuring his son had a life like that which John had never had himself. Jacquelyn had begged him to marry her. She resented his feelings of love for Jo Anna. John knew if he married Jacquelyn and moved to France he couldn't afford her lifestyle. The position that he had with the Bovier's gave him access to the money that kind of life took. Later when his son was hurt on his motor cycle the hospital bills had been unreal. As long as Jo Anna's father was alive, he capitalized on him, being a rich senator who had no desire to confess to a rape of a juvenal, in which she had became pregnant. That had been a breeze. When he died things got tough.

Miranda got in the way, he thought. If only she had left well enough alone. But no, she got nossy. She had seen Jacquelyn with him the day of the event, he still had a hard time saying murder, that is something you read about in movies. They had been arguing outside the Pinetree Lounge. Miranda had surprised them.

Jacquelyn had flown in from Paris and rented a car. She had found him at the Pinetree Lounge and waited for him to come out.

"I want my gun," she said. "I'm going to finish this once and for all, this obsession of yours with Jo Anna has got to stop. Your son needs you. Don't you get it, your son needs you." Jacquelyn took the 357 Magnum out from under John's front seat. Got back into the rented Lincoln and pulled out. Miranda had watched as he followed Jacquelyn out of the parking lot.

If only, John thought, if he would have caught up to her sooner. If only he'd would have married her. Maybe Jo Anna would be alive. He tried to stop her, but she struggled with him and then Joe got in the way.

Now Miranda, poor kid. The only thing she was guilty of was trying to help him. She was too good a listener, too good a listener. But she was curious and asked too many questions.

Now he had to find Lawrence. He was the only one now that could hurt his family. Then he would finish up his paper work at Bovier, quit his job and move to Paris and marry Jacquelyn. They would be a family at last. As soon as John Ash got off the airplane, he called Lawrence and set up a meeting at the Pinetree Lounge.

The Boston Globe morning paper placed a prominent picture of a man on it's front cover, and a phone number to call if anyone knew where he was.

"Finally, it's about time." he said after his call from Mr. Ash. "He finally talked Adam into giving me the One million dollars. Maybe the thing in the mall did scare him a him a little." The meeting time was set for three p.m. at the Pinetree Lounge.

"Mr. Pinetree read the news in his office and returned to the bar when Lawrence walked in. He observed as the man seated himself at the bar and asked for a double Royal Crown.

"Where's Miranda?" He asked Dorrie. He laid his head in his arms on the table. "Dang," he said, "I need some valium." He grabbed Dorrie's arm and his hand was shaking so that he put his other out to stop it.

"Excuse me, I'll be right back." Dorrie said as she moved closer to her boss. Mr. Pinetree," she said, "He's looking for a fix. He's asking for valium."

"Be right back, keep him busy," Mr. Pinetree went to his office and pushed the police code.

"We're on the way. What's the problem?" the officer on the other end asked as his partner turned the squad car around and headed toward the Pinetree Lounge.

"I believe we have the guy who's picture was plastered all over the morning newspaper. You know the guy who killed that society babe, Jo Anna Bovier. By the way he is looking for drugs. We don't do that here you know," he informed them.

"Be right there," the officer said.

Two big guys in police uniforms walked into the front of Pinetree Lounge and within minutes had Lawrence Bovier in a squad car. There were no problems, just one sobbing man-child.

"I want my dad. I want my mom. I want my dad. I want my mom. Please help me. Help mom, help dad." He kept whimpering like a child.

When they arrived at the Police Station, J. D. Hanson knew who he was from the profile composite. He picked up the phone and called Adam Bovier.

"I'll be right down sir," Adam said. "Even though he hates me, I'm all he has left."

"A fathers love," J. D. sighed when he hung up.

Suddenly things changed. The police officer shouted at his partner. "We need to move him to a hospital, guys. He's going into shock. "I've called a rescue unit, it's on it's way." Just then the vehicle backed into the drive.

The medics tied Lawrence on a gurney, and carried him out. They were almost to the van when shots rang out. "Dang, he's been shot." the driver hollered. J. D. and two of his officers pulled their guns and scouted the area.

The medics were in a panic. "One of them shouted, "He's bleeding badly, let me in there with him, and you get us to the General Hospital" He jumped in by the cot, someone slammed the door and they sped to the hospital.

"He's gone," J. D. said to his officers. They had heard the car take off before they made it clear of the small wooded area behind the prison.

Adam pulled in just in time to see the ambulance pull away. He got the report and followed his son to the hospital.

As they wheeled Lawrence into the emergency room the medics had already administered stabilizing drugs, and were working on stopping the bleeding.

"He's my son," Adam told the intern on duty. Lawrence opened his eyes and looked at his dad.

"You're here, I hoped you would come," he said before the sedatives took over and he closed his eyes in sleep.

Adam touched his son on the shoulder and gave it a squeeze. Oh, how he had longed to know his son as a child and even as a teenager, but he had been rebuffed. First by his mother and later by Lawrence himself. He remembered the night he had found him standing over Jo Anna. If it hadn't been for the gun in his hand, Adam would have been convinced he had seen compassion on his son's face. He appeared almost gentle as he had touched her face. "A man-child who never found his place," Adam said. John found it hard to believe that his flesh could kill someone, but his blood wasn't the only blood to flow through his veins.

After about an hour the intern came back looking for Adam. "We are preparing him for surgery," Mr. Bovier. "The bullet is lodged in a very precarious position, but none the less it has to be removed or he will bleed to death. Dr. Ferenza has been called and the operating room is ready when he arrives." He paused to look closely at Adam. "I've heard of your situation, and it really has got to be tough, Mr. Bovier. Will you stay?" He asked Adam.

"I'm all he has, so yes I'll be here." Adam waited until he left and then he called home to tell Jessica the situation.

"I'll stay until he is out of trouble, if he comes out." Adam told Jessica. "I'll rest here in the waiting room." Adam was so tired and so distraught, and he felt so disloyal, although he knew Jo Anna would want him here, if there was anything he could do for his son. In his gut he wanted to believe in his son.

Adam wondered how long John would be gone. He leads a double life, it would seem. He had become so secretive. Lately, especially since Jo Anna was gone, John had become especially moody, anxious, almost hostile, Adam thought.

Finally Adam put the pillow on the couch under his head, and put his feet up. This is going to be a long night, he thought, what will tomorrow bring.

Adam was there, he was there for me. Lawrence thought his father didn't like him. 'He doesn't want us, can't you see, he's only interested in money, that's why he married Moneybag's daughter.' He had heard that so many times. On special days, or when he played ball, he wanted his dad to be there. After while he pretended he didn't care.

"We're going to put you to sleep now Mr. Bovier. Count to ten."

"One, two, three,——. He was there—He was there, my dad was there, four——."

Chapter Twenty One

The aroma of fresh coffee brewing in the galley of the giant aircraft, flying from Paris France to the United States, reminded Scott that soon he would be faced with delivering evidence against Adam's lifetime associate and friend, John Ash and his mistress, and the mother of John's teenage son. Their arrival into Logan Airport in Boston was scheduled for nine a.m. The clink clink of the food trays being placed on the carts made Scott hungry.

Connie was sleeping peacefully propped on her pillow against the window. Her long legs propped up on the seat beside her. Scott looked at her golden hair she had pulled up and held with a clip. Soft tendrils dropped gently over her cheeks and forehead. A natural beauty he thought. Scott thought about the newspaper Tim had handed him. He pulled out his briefcase and looked in it for something to read. The headline article: Girl crushed to death in fall from terminal ramp.

Meo Rose

    His eye caught the caption of the girls long red hair and her arms flailed around her. He knew it was Miranda. "Oh no," Scott's breath quickened.

    "What," Connie sat up and looked at the caption Scott was focused on.

    "That's Miranda," Scott replied. "She's the girl I told you traveled with John Ash to Paris. As soon as we arrive I'll give Tim a call and let him know. We'll stop by the Pinetree Lounge and tell them, they'll know how to notify her parents. How sad," Scott squeezed Connie's hand. He knew he needed to get Connie to safe haven and keep her there, until this thing was pinned down.

    Shortly coffee was served and they were enjoying an excellent omelet, ham and banana bread with honey. The next hour went by quickly. "Welcome to Boston, Ladies and Gentlemen," the personable Flight Attendant announced. Soon they were headed out of the airport toward Scott's automobile. Scott reached for his phone to turn it on. As he did it rang, starling him. "Scott here," he said.

    "Hey it's J. D. all hells broke lose here, where you at?"

    "It's been a blast in Paris too. You go first, what's new? Scott asked.

    "We picked up Lawrence Bovier last night at the Pinetree Lounge. Got a call from the owner. Seems Larry boy was looking for Miranda to get some drugs. She wasn't there and he became hysterical. The owner recognized him from the picture in the news, and reported that also. When they got him to the police station, he had the shakes so bad they had to call the medics to get him to the hospital. Three guards, mind you, and two medics. Someone called out his name. 'Hey Larry,' he said, and then sunk two bullets into his ribs and left arm." J. D. Hanson was wound up tighter then a yoyo.

"Did they get the guy?" Scott had an idea who it was. Larry would have known too much.

"Nope, he got away, before we could even get a tail on him. Larry's at General Hospital now. Last I heard he had lost a lot of blood, and they took him to surgery. I think he'll live. His dad, Adam Bovier is with him." J. D. responded.

"So you didn't get to question him?" Scott wanted to tell J. D. about Connie, but he'd just take her in to make her statement. "I'll be in after I go by the Pinetree Lounge. Miranda is not coming back and I need to talk to the owner anyway."

When they walked into the police station a while later Scott introduced Connie to everyone. "This is a star witness so take good care of her." She was questioned and taped again. "I think it is almost over," Scott told J D. "Connie was the maid for Jacquelyn B. Ansley for the last two years. John Ash had the 357 Magnum in his possession, and Jacquelyn Ansley was in the United States on the fifteenth of June. One or both of them had to be in the garden that night. John wouldn't marry Jacquelyn because he was still in love with Jo Anna. Jacquelyn had a real hatred for Jo Anna, so I think we could prove she had motive."

J. D. was ready to pick Ash up. "I think we have enough to get a warrant for John Ash's arrest. We'll question him and go from there."

John Ash sat behind his mahogany desk. An open bottle of Royal Crown in one hand and a double shot glass in the other. "So this is what a man's life comes to." Some have it all, like Adam, he thought. Two unfinished letters lay on the desk in front of him. One was to his son Ashley. One was to Adam. Jacquelyn would understand, and she would have to live with the memories of that night the rest of her life. John picked up the phone and rang General Hospital.

"This is a friend of the Bovier's, and I'd like to check on Lawrence Bovier's condition," John prompted the receptionist.

"I'll connect you to that station, one moment please." she replied.

"Yes sir, you were checking on Lawrence Bovier. He is in recovery. The doctor is talking to Adam Bovier now. Would you like to give Mr. Bovier a message?" the nurse asked.

John thought a minute and then, "no." he said. Recovery room, John thought, by tomorrow morning he'll be talking about what he saw in the garden that night. "It's over." John picked up the phone and tried to call the Ansley residence in Paris. No answer. Where are they? He left a message. "Jacquelyn, it's over, I failed. Please take care of our son." John opened his safe, laid the 357 Magnum on his desk and loaded it. He locked his door, sit down at his desk, and finished the two letters. Then he filled his shot glass and waited.

Scott took Connie to Hatley House and then he went back to the Police Station. The warrant was ready for John Ash's arrest and he wanted to be there when they picked him up.

J. D. and two of his officers stood in front of Mr. John Ash's receptionist's desk. "Can you ring John and tell him we are here and would like to see him," J. D. showed her his card.

She rang the intercom, "Mr. Ash some police officer's are here to see you," she told John.

They heard the shot, and were quickly at the door, ramming it open. "Call an ambulance," Scott shouted at the girl, but he knew it was too late.

Scott and J. D. found Adam still waiting for his son to come out of the recovery room. They had good news and they had bad news.

"Lawrence was not guilty of killing Jo Anna and Joe Santana. As far as they could discern he was not even guilty of Donna Mavis's death. She was a suicide, the state of California had confirmed that from an eye witness. His psychiatrist's report said his last sessions with Lawrence showed a desire to finally see his father and his sister, Jessica." Scott explained as gently as possible.

"You mean I've been judging him as if guilty all this time, I thought he was getting even with me. I think I'll have some making up to do. But who then?" Adam asked.

"John Ash," Scott handed Adam the letter.

John took the letter and read it to them. 'Jacquelyn has always been jealous of my love for Jo Anna. She took the gun and said she was going to handle it once and for all. I followed her and she was waiting for Jo Anna who was on the porch of the cottage. Jo Anna had Adam's gun in her hand. Joe told her he didn't need it, to take it back. Jacquelyn raised the gun to shoot, but I struggled with her and the gun went off and the bullet hit Jo Anna. She fell, and Joe picked it up and shot twice over our heads, and I shot him. When I turned around someone moved by the gazebo. I fled, and I didn't know who it was until you told me Lawrence was there. You must have found him when he picked up the gun.' Adam hung his head. He couldn't go on. He laid the letter by his side, and sat with his hands covering his face. "It's over," he finally said, and life goes on.

After J. D. and Scott left, Adam picked up the letter and read on. John had a son? Adam realized how little he had kept up with his friend. Friend, he stole from me!! Adam thought. He could almost forgive John when he read about John's sons accident and repeated surgeries over the last five years. He would make an attempt to meet this Jacquelyn and John Ash's son. He'd make sure they were taken care of. Jo Anna would want him to, he knew that. Why hadn't John just confided in him. I would've helped him, Adam thought. It was more than Adam could even comprehend. Had John hated him all those years, because of Jo Anna. How can we know what another man is thinking if his pride gets in the way.

Dr. Ferenza found Adam deep in thought. "Your son is asking for you, Mr. Bovier. We are going to take him to his own room soon and if you want to you can stay with him. He's still not out of the woods, but he has a good chance." The doctor sat down and explained the prognosis. When he left Adam called home and told Jessica he would be home in the morning. He wanted to stay with his son in case he woke up. There were some things he needed to say.

Chapter Twenty Two

The guests would start arriving about five pm. Tiffany and Jessica were spending the morning setting out bouquets on the tables that were set around the pool area. Mary and James had hired extras to help serve and they were being trained by Mary. They dressed in maroon peasant looking dresses, scalloped aprons that had wide black cummerbunds.

Spanish dancers would be entertaining, and singers would serenade the guests while they ate And walkways had been set to span the pool, like little bridges. These would be used by the dancers during their performances. Gazebo archways were decorated with hanging wisteria and roses, on each corner of the dance floor that had been set in place. A stage for the band had been elevated with decorations streaming down from the corner poles.

Meo Rose

Jo Lynn had been given one of the guest rooms, from which a balcony opened to the pool area. She had slept in and now found her way to the gardens. Tiffany made her comfortable, by conversing with her in Spanish. Mary brought them coffee and brunch to the pool area. After that they all walked through the garden and over to the little cottage. Albert was working in the shed, so they ventured into the shed to see the big chest that was full of toys and souvenirs of Jo Anna's life. Tiffany interpreted whenever Jessica messed up on her Spanish.

"Where is Al?" Jessica asked Albert.

"Doing some shopping." he answered.

"We're going to show Jo Lynn some pictures inside, Tiffany took Jo Lynn's arm and showed her into the cottage.

"Like me," Jo Lynn said pointing to herself and the semblance of Jo Anna she saw on the side table.

"And Me," Jessica said pointing to herself.

"And Me," Tiffany said pointing to herself.

They all laughed, put their arms around each other and walked back through the gardens. Tiffany made them laugh when she demonstrated how she had danced and how Ryan had caught her standing on the bench, practicing a bow.

"Princess Dianna, I think it is time for an afternoon nap, so we will be refreshed for the ball tonight." Jessica told her. "Let's all meet at three thirty and dress together in my chambers." Jessica took Jo Lynn's arm and they walked to the Hatley House together. Without her Spanish attire Jo Lynn looked even more than ever like Jo Anna had, Jessica thought. Joe Santana would have been proud of this granddaughter as well, Jessica thought. Tonight will indeed be a tribute to the Santanas.——.

The guests had been arriving, and Adam was being the perfect host. Drinks were being served in the gardens. Jessica and Tiffany were putting the last minute sparkles on Jo Lynn's hair. Their escorts were waiting by the threshold of the stairs in the grand hall. Tiffany would go first and today they would walk all two flights. A hush filled the air as they started their descent down the stairs.

Ryan watched Tiffany, his eyes beaming with pride. The baby blue bodice fell off her shoulders just ever so slightly. The purity of face, and the beauty of youth, was manifest as she gracefully lifted her long skirt so as to traverse the two flights. Her long black hair flowed behind her. Tiny ribbons of matching blue were caught up in strands to flow and twinkle in the lights. Ryan looked stunning in his white tuxedo. He had chosen a baby blue shirt and black bow tie. As Tiffany took his hand, everyone clapped there approval.

Eyes moved once more to the stairs, Jessica moved forward and drifted down the steps so familiar from of her youth. It was obvious to all that she had been here before, and now assumed her place as Mistress of Hatley House. A golden shimmering, fitted gown is what she had worn tonight. It was simple and chic. Jo Anna would be proud, Adam thought. He

Meo Rose

smiled as he watched as his daughter reached for Al's hand at the steps end. "I love you," Al whispered in her ear, as they moved on, and she ignored the clapping, her face was beaming.

Adam was there to escort Jo Lynn. As she stepped into the view a gasp was heard by the guests. For most this was the first time they had seen Jo Lynn. Tonight she had opted to dress more Americano, as she put it. She wore black, in mourning for the grandfather and the sister she had never known. The resemblance was obvious. Her hair was pulled down from a center part and wound low at the base of her neck, a style that Jo Anna had often wore. Everyone clapped as Adam took her hand and led the guests to the gardens. Every one was seated the entertainment began and the first course of the meal was served.

When they had finished eating, Al took Jessica by the hand, "Let's walk."

The band was playing and the young group was slowly filtering to the dance floor. Adam and Jo Lynn were seriously talking. He could converse in her language easily, the diplomat that he was. Albert had joined them. It wouldn't be long, Jessica thought, before Jo Lynn's English would be fluent.

"How's it going?" Al asked the Hughes, setting with another couple who were asked to chaperone the party. They all thanked Jessica for her hospitality. This was an event that the young members of the Botanical Society looked forward to. They hoped it would continue to be one of their charities.

Al led Jessica through the garden. Deliberately he paused at the pond where they had dropped the stone, only a few weeks ago. He turned Jessica to face him and kissed her fervently. "Did you mean it when you said you would marry me?" he whispered.

"Uhhuh," she answered.

Al reached in his pocket then and opened a small box. The diamond that he slipped on her finger, sparkled as brightly as the tears in her eyes. "I hope those are tears of happiness," he said.

Jessica was speechless. Finally she uttered, "I think I will just write about it in a journal. "That's it, I'll call it Jessica's Journal."

About the Author

Meo Rose was born and raised in Michigan. She now resides with her husband Don in the D'arbonne Lake area of northern Louisiana. A retired flight attendant, Meo says the places she has traveled and the people she met on her flights from area to area greatly influence her stories. Meo started her writing as a children's writer. She is a graduate of 'The Institute of Children's Literature.' She has four grown daughters, twelve grandchildren, and three great grandchildren. They supply Meo with an endless supply of real life situations to write about.

Printed in the United States
19474LVS00001B/217-312